Stan Barstow was born and still lives in the West Riding of Yorkshire. He is married and has a son and a daughter. After working in the engineering industry, mainly as a draughtsman, he became a full-time writer in 1962.

His first novel, *A Kind of Loving*, was published in 1960. Since then he has published three volumes of short stories and nine more novels, including *A Raging Calm*, *Joby*, *A Brother's Tale*, *Just You Wait and See* and *Give Us This Day*. His work is read and studied widely in schools. He has been published in the United States and translated into nine European languages. The Open University has conferred on Stan Barstow an Honorary Degree of Master of Arts.

He has won The Royal Television Society Award for Writers on two occasions and The Writers' Guild and BAFTA Awards for his television dramatisations, notably, *Joby*, *A Raging Calm* and for Winifred Holtby's *South Riding*.

A Kind of Loving became a feature film (director John Schlesinger) and a ten-part television serial. *A Brother's Tale* was also televised in three episodes.

Author photograph by Neil Barstow

Give Us This Day

Stan Barstow

BLACK SWAN

GIVE US THIS DAY

A BLACK SWAN BOOK 0 552 99434 0

Originally published in Great Britain by
Michael Joseph Ltd

PRINTING HISTORY
Michael Joseph edition published 1989
Black Swan edition published 1990

This book is set in 11/12pt Mallard
by Busby The Printers Ltd, Exeter

Black Swan Books are published by
Transworld Publishers Ltd, 61–63 Uxbridge Road,
Ealing, London W5 5SA, in Australia by
Transworld Publishers (Australia) Pty. Ltd,
15–23 Helles Avenue, Moorebank, NSW 2170,
and in New Zealand by Transworld Publishers
(N.Z.) Ltd, Cnr. Moselle and Waipareira Avenues,
Henderson, Auckland.

Made and printed in Great Britain by
Cox & Wyman Ltd, Reading, Berks.

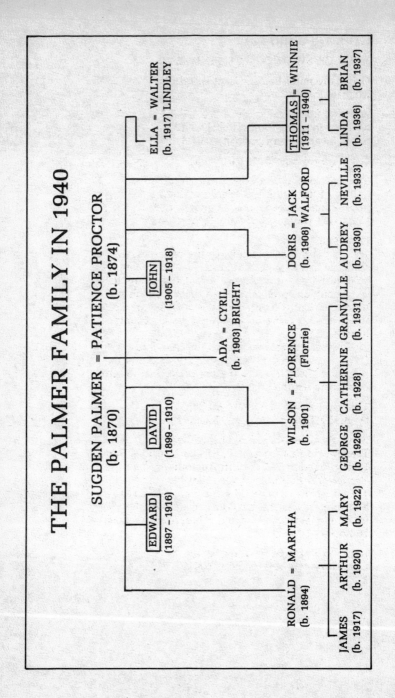

THE PALMER FAMILY IN 1940

Part One

One

1

A fine Saturday morning in late September 1940, and Ella was playing the half-shift from the mill because her husband was coming home on a weekend pass. Bathed, her hair washed, with her yellow ribbon, her lemon-coloured gloves, and only a thin cardigan over a sleeveless dress in the surprising warmth of the approaching noonday, it struck her that she was virtually a replica of that younger reluctant self who had gone out for the first time with Walter, when he had taken her to the summer feast before the war. Except, she thought, that I know a few things now that I didn't know then.

There were two little lasses hanging about on the causeway edge ahead of her as she walked down towards Daker Junction railway station, and as she drew near she could see that one of them was upset about something, her shoulders heaving and sobs tearing out of her like croup. 'Whatever's the matter?' The other girl looked at her helplessly. 'There's nowt as bad as all that, surely.'

'She's frightened her dad'll leather her,' the crying girl's friend said.

'Leather her? What for?'

'I've lost his tripe,' the crying girl managed, and Ella for a second didn't think she had heard her rightly.

'Did you say his tripe?' But the girl was overcome by her sobbing again and Ella had to ask her friend. 'Did she say tripe?'

The girl nodded. 'We've been to fetch her dad some tripe for his tea.'

'Well, where is it, then?' She noticed now that the

crying girl was holding on to a piece of white wrapping-paper and a crumpled sheet of the *Empire News*. 'Was it in there?'

'Yes.'

'Where is it now, then?'

The crying girl cast her gaze down and Ella, following it, saw that they were, all three, standing round a grated drain.

'You don't mean it's . . . ?'

The crying girl spoke again. 'We were aleckin' about, Missus, an' all at once it slipped out of the paper. T'next thing I knew it wa' through t'bars and . . . I don't know what I'm goin' to do. I daren't go home an' tell him. He'll bray me till I'm black an' blue.'

'He will an' all,' her friend said. 'He's got a right bad temper. He gets goin' over nowt at all, sometimes.'

Ella peered down through the bars of the grate to the blue-black liquid below. Something pale floated just under its surface.

'Can you lift t'grate up, Missus?' the friend asked. 'I've seen lads do it.'

'Nay,' Ella said, 'this is set in wi' muck. We'll never shift this. An' even if we did he'd very likely end up with typhoid if he ate owt that'd been down there.'

This set the crying girl off again and an elderly man passing on the other side of the road stopped and called across.

'What the hummer's up wi' that bairn?'

'Don't tell him, Missus,' the crying girl got out, and Ella called back, 'She'll be all right in a minute.'

She wouldn't, though, unless something was done.

'Have you got any money to buy some more?'

'No.'

'How much was there?'

'Two penn'orth.'

Ella took her purse out of her handbag. 'Well, look, see. Stop your roarin' and listen to me. Do you know who I am?'

'You're Granville Palmer's auntie.'

'Oh, you know our Granville, do you? You're not old enough to be in his class, are you?'

'No. He's Standard Four. We're only Standard Three.'

'They tell me he's very clever. Is that right?'

'Ooh, yes. He's allus top.'

'He's funny, though, as well,' the other girl said.

'I know,' Ella said. 'I've heard some of his jokes. Well, look, I'm Mrs Lindley. That's me married name. Do you know where I live?'

'Next door to t'Masons Arms.'

'Hmm. It seems there's nowt you don't know. Apart from how to get some more tripe for your dad. Now don't start all that again,' she said as the girl's shoulders heaved once more. She took each of them by the arm.

'If I lend you tuppence to buy some more will you promise faithful to pay me back?'

'Ooh, yes, Missus.'

'Righto.' She opened her purse. 'Here you are. What do they call you, by the way?'

'Mary Butterworth,' the crying girl said.

'Mavis Bright,' said her friend.

'Bright? One of me sisters is married to a chap called Bright,' Ella said. 'You haven't got an Uncle Cyril, by any chance, have you?'

'No.'

'No. We'd surely have known if you had. Nowt to hide in that. Anyway, look, if you go and buy some more, and . . .'

'I daren't go meself,' Mary said.

'Why not?'

'He'll wonder why I've been twice and happen mention it to somebody.'

'Oh . . .' Ella stood irresolute. 'I've spent enough time on this. I'm supposed to be meeting me husband off a train an' I haven't seen him for over a month. Is t'shop still open?'

'It wa' ten minutes since.'

'Well, if he's shut in the meantime you'll just have to go home and own up, won't you? Lasses. Laikin' about

11

till you drop your dad's tripe down a grate. I never
heard owt like it.'

'Oh, hurry up, Missus,' Mary begged, on the edge of
tears again.

'Was it just plain tripe?' Ella asked. 'Nowt fancy, like
elder or cowheel?'

'Just tripe.'

'Right.'

Ella walked round the corner and found the small
dark man with a twisted back still in his lock-up shed
of a shop which he opened only at irregular intervals,
when he had something to sell.

'Just in time,' he told her.

Ella carried the tripe back to the two girls and stood
over them with a solemn face.

'Now, listen. I shall expect you to bring me that tuppence as soon as you've saved it out of your spend.
D'you understand?'

'Ooh, yes, Missus. Thanks ever so much. You won't
tell anybody, will you?'

'No, I won't. You just bring me that money and I'll
know I've done the right thing. I can't play the Good
Samaritan to everybody 'at drops their father's tripe
down a grate, y'know.'

She laughed over that when she had left them. Chuck-
ling out loud she drew a curious look from a couple
waiting to cross the road as she drew level.

2

Walter had to change trains at Retford and again at
Calderford. His last train would eventually cross the
Pennines into Lancashire. There was a well-to-do looking
man and a woman with two children – a boy and a
girl – waiting with luggage and Ella wondered if they
were going on a late holiday. She was reminded of her
wedding day and trundling up the valley in snow, on
the way to a Blackpool honeymoon. She wondered

why the man wasn't in uniform, then thought that they had probably not yet reached his age group. On the other hand, he looked big enough to be on work of national importance. Funny the things that made a man like that stand out. It was in his choice of clothes (not necessarily new or what you usually thought of as smart), in his grooming, the way he carried himself, the way – Ella realized as she caught a word or two – he used the long 'a', saying 'barth' and 'larst' and 'parst' as nobody did round these parts unless they had had the local speech trained out of them. A man with authority. A leader. Send a man like that for air-crew training in Canada and he wouldn't be home early.

It had quietened Walter down, that, made him a lot more reflective. Ella knew that it would have been less damaging to his self-esteem if he had never been accepted for training, rather than being accepted and then thrown off the course. He could have consoled himself with the thought that there were only too many young men far better qualified than he was ahead of him in the queue. As it was, Ella could not rid her mind of the conviction that somebody, somewhere had made a mistake in the first place; though she never gave Walter the slightest hint of it and tried hard not to let him feel a failure. And she knew how best to please him. She had married him against her better judgement, thinking herself in love with another man whom she had met only briefly. But in her attempt to do her duty by him she had opened a vein of sensuality in herself which she had not known she possessed, and she took Walter to her sometimes with an evident passion that surprised and delighted him.

After strolling the length of the island platform, Ella sat down beside a girl holding a tiny baby. As it kicked its feet in their knitted bootees and made gurgling sounds, the girl turned her round, pale-skinned face to Ella and pursed her small rosebud mouth in a smile. She had thick ankles and wore heavy lisle stockings despite the mild weather which Ella had welcomed as

13

allowing her to save her own stockings and walk out bare-legged.

'Have you the right time?' the girl asked and Ella leaned forward in an attempt to see the station clock which hung, out of view here, between the two platforms. 'Just coming up to twelve, I believe.'

'He allus knows,' the girl said, looking into the baby's face as his wet sounds hardened into something like the beginning of protest. 'He knows it's time he was fed.'

'Is he good as a rule?' Ella asked.

'Except when he wants his titty,' the girl said. 'Then he lets you know. He lets everybody know.'

She was wearing a beret, pulled squarely over mouse-brown hair, and a navy-blue jacket and skirt.

'Are you going to feed him now?'

'There'll be ructions if I don't.'

'Well, I'm sure nobody minds.'

'I'm sure we don't mind who minds, do we, Colin?' the girl said. 'We don't give tuppence who minds.' She unbuttoned her blouse and palmed her left breast. The skin was taut and blue-veined over its fullness. The baby's mouth smacked about the large brown nipple, found centre and sucked it in.

'That should keep him quiet for a while,' Ella said. Plenty of time for herself, she thought. No rush. But, watching, she found herself envying the girl the sensation of that demanding mouth. She must, she told herself, be on special guard this weekend. Her father and mother liked grandchildren well enough when they came on visits; but a baby in the house night and day would be a very different matter. Besides, Ella wanted to carry on working for some time yet. What she saved from her wages was to help in getting them their own place. And a better place than any of the others had managed, or she'd know the reason why.

'I'm meeting my husband,' she told the girl with the feeding baby. 'He's coming on the seven minutes past twelve train. He's in the RAF. He's stationed in Lincolnshire. We're lucky, him being so near. It means

14

he can get the odd weekend pass between proper leaves. I don't suppose it'll last for ever so we're making the best of it while it does.'

The man with the long a's barked a command at the small boy, who had ventured too near the edge of the platform.

'Is it your husband you're waiting for?' Ella asked the girl.

'Yes.'

'What's he in – RAF, Army . . .?'

'He's a soldier.'

'Has he far to come?'

'Farther than yours.'

'How long is it since you've seen him?'

'Oh . . .' The girl frowned.

'It's been over a month with us,' Ella said. 'Even though he's quite near.'

'Do you ever forget what he looks like?' the girl asked, and Ella, surprised, said 'No'. She didn't. Not Walter. But there had been moments when she couldn't summon up Howard's face. She said as a thought struck her, 'How old is the baby?'

'Colin, his name is. He's nine weeks.'

'And has his father never . . . ?'

'No,' the girl said.

'Oh! Well, he has got a treat in store. Heavens! You must be excited. Him as well.'

The bell had rung and now the small boy was signalling the approach of the train with an excited little jig in which he would have involved his older sister had she not haughtily fended him off.

Ella stood up. Walter waved to her as he leaned out of the lowered window and felt for the door-handle. His hair had always been stubborn and RAF barbers did nothing to help it stick down. But he looked fit, trimmed a bit in weight, his fair complexion rich with colour. He brought a small case out with him and swung it behind her as he threw his arms round Ella and kissed her full on the mouth.

'By, but you're a sight for sore eyes.'

' "Goin' to t'vicar's garden party?" ' she said, quoting and teasing him.

He remembered and grinned, quoting back, ' "You want a slut, Walter Lindley, you go and find one." ' He kissed her again and spoke into her ear. 'If you knew what I'm thinking just now.'

'Oh, I can guess.'

He laughed and took her arm to lead her off the platform. Then he exclaimed, 'Hang on a tick. I'm forgettin' summat.' He located the compartment he had travelled in and reached a brown-paper parcel off the seat. 'Summat for you.'

'What is it?' It gave to the touch.

'I hope it's parachute silk. Somebody shoved it under me arm at the last minute.'

'What's it for?'

'Making underwear.'

'For you?'

'For *you*, woman, for you.'

'How did you get it?'

'I did a bloke a favour.'

They were at the entrance to the tunnel-ramp. Ella glanced back. The girl with the baby still sat on the seat. The guard was walking along closing doors on the train.

Ella said, 'Oh, don't tell me he hasn't come! Oh, that poor lass!'

'What's up?'

'She was waiting for her husband. He's never seen the baby.'

'Oh, happen she's got her train time wrong,' Walter said. 'Happen he has. Happen he's missed his connection. Happen they were late getting out of camp. Happen they suddenly cancelled all leave. Happen he's on his way to Timbuctoo.' He took her arm again. 'Come on. It's a miracle anybody's on time anywhere these days. We're among the lucky ones. For now.'

'Did you hear what I said, though?' Ella asked.

'What was that?' Walter got out his travel warrant as they reached the top of the slope.

'I said she was telling me that her husband had never seen the baby.' The ticket-collector looked at her over the head of an elderly man who couldn't find his ticket. 'Is there another train soon?' Ella asked him.

'Another from Calderford in twenty minutes.' He glanced at Walter's warrant as the elderly man moved on. 'Have you been talking to Valerie?'

'Valerie?'

'Young woman with a baby.'

'Oh, yes. I was just telling me husband how disappointed she must be.'

The ticket-collector had freckled hands and red hairs grew out of his nostrils. 'She waits for at least one train every day,' he said. 'Nobody ever gets off for her.'

'What d'you mean?'

'If she stops too long her mother comes for her.'

Ella looked round as she felt the boards vibrate under their feet. The girl was pushing her pram up the tunnel. They stood and waited. Ella felt dismay yawn in her stomach. The girl lifted her chin and stared them out.

'What are you lookin' at? There's nowt to stare for.'

'See you later, Valerie,' the ticket-collector said as she walked out into the street.

'He's not been killed, has he?' Ella asked, and the man said,

'Oh, no, nowt like that.' He was keen to tell them about her.

'Completely normal, she was,' he said. 'All her chairs at home. Went to Birmingham to see a friend what had moved from here. Turned out there were some soldiers. Valerie went off with 'em to a party. Her pal lost her and ended up reporting it. The police brought Valerie home nearly a week later. Nobody could get a straight tale out of her. They don't know to this day exactly what did happen, except it soon came to light 'at she was expecting. And' – the ticket-collector tapped his

·17

temple with his forefinger – 'she's been eleven-pence ha'penny in the shilling ever since.'

'So she comes and sits and waits for t'bairn's father to arrive on a train?'

'Hardly ever misses a day.'

'There's some right bastards about,' Walter said as they walked up the street. The girl with the pram was ahead of them, taking her time. 'You meet 'em as you move around. Doesn't half open your eyes, service life. Mind you,' he went on, 'you take even an ordinary decent sort of a bloke, with a few pints inside him and a lass he's not likely to see again . . . He doesn't allus behave like he does in his own backyard.'

'Well, he ought to,' Ella said, and Walter glanced sideways at her, impressed by the vehemence of her tone.

'What he ought to do and what he does do aren't allus the same thing.'

'Men away from home,' Ella said, 'they think they can do what they like.'

'Some do,' Walter admitted. 'Some don't. And it's not every woman 'at needs holding down, either.'

'There's no need to be crude about it. That poor lass has had her life ruined.'

'I'm not gettin' into an argument about her,' Walter said. 'It wasn't me what raped her.'

'I feel as though I want to run after her and say something.'

'Like what?'

'I don't know. But look, see. Oh, Walter, I *shall* have to go to her.'

'What's up now?'

'Her suspender's broken.'

The girl walked on, seemingly oblivious, as the stocking on her left leg sagged and concertina-ed into wrinkles round her calf. But even as Ella made to leave Walter's side an older woman stepped out of a narrow side-street and spoke to the girl, taking her protectively by the arm. The woman glanced down. The girl stopped and stood still. As Ella and Walter drew level the woman

18

was on one knee, her hands feeling for the suspender-fastening under the girl's skirt.

Ella said 'Good morning' and the woman nodded. 'I've been talkin' to your, er, your . . .'

'My daughter,' the woman said.

'She's got a lovely little boy.'

'Yes.' The woman was taking in Walter's uniform. 'Is this your husband?'

'Yes.'

'You want to look after him.'

'Oh, I do,' Ella said.

' "Oh, I do",' Walter mimicked, when they had left the mother and daughter. 'Nobody thinks to ask *me*.'

'Could you say any different?'

'Chance 'ud be a fine thing.'

'Whenever have you swallowed a complaint?'

'Now you're tryin' to make out 'at you know what I *don't* say.'

'I've allus had quite enough on with what you *do* say, Walter Lindley. That's plenty for anybody to be goin' on with.'

'I'll say no more, then,' Walter said.

'No, don't, else we'll find we're squabbling.'

'Why should we do that?'

'I don't know. Sometimes you're into it afore you know it.' It was as though the girl with the baby had somehow come between them, making them both touchy. She took his arm. 'I didn't come to meet you in that frame of mind.'

'I should hope not.'

'I said I didn't.'

'I heard you.'

'Walter.' Ella stopped and turned to face him. 'Walter, we're gettin' cross-threaded some road, and we haven't the time for it.'

Walter glanced over his shoulder. There was a pub across the road, The Forge Inn. He said, 'Let's go and have a drink.' Ella wrinkled her nose. 'They've got a snug; you don't have to be among t'men.'

19

'Me mam's cookin' a hot dinner for us. If you want a drink can't you get a bottle from t'Masons?'

Walter scowled. He looked again at the open door of the pub. 'You go on,' he said. 'I'll be up in a quarter of an hour.'

Ella couldn't believe it. 'Nay, Walter, you're surely not sending me home on me own.'

'You can come in with me.'

'Me mam's got a dinner in t'oven. It'll spoil. It's not fair when she's gone to the trouble.'

Walter said, 'Look, I'm under orders every bloody minute I'm away. I'll be buggered if I'm going to be ruled by anybody else's timetable when I'm at home.'

She could have pointed out that he wasn't going to his own home, but somebody else's where he lived for the present, while on leave. But she quickly thought better of that and stood in a moment of frowning indecision before saying, 'All right,' and making as if to start across the road. But Walter caught her arm and checked her. 'No, you're right. We'll go home and have some dinner.'

Ella now wanted to say – and could recall a time when she would not have been able to resist saying – 'Make your mind up.' But she did resist and knew herself to be right in not giving way to petty irritation. A fine weekend this was going to be if someone didn't take it in hand. She had never known Walter so fractious. Not, that was, since before they were married, when her own peevishness had sometimes goaded him. She asked quietly, trying to keep all suspicion of provocation out of her voice,

'Is there summat worrying you, Walter?'

He hung his head and scraped his foot. It was a gesture she had come to know well, but had not seen for some time; the gesture of a proud man unsure of his ground. 'Bloody hell!' she heard him breathe. 'I'm doing it all wrong.'

They walked on. 'If me mam hasn't got it ready to put on the table,' she said, 'I'll go round to t'Masons

20

for a drink with you.' She felt the pressure of his arm on hers.

'It's all right,' he said. 'I wanted to talk for a minute or two, that's all.'

'What do you want to do this afternoon?' she asked him.

'What had you in mind?'

'Well, I expect you'll want to go and see your dad, and your Nellie sometime. Then I thought we might go down either Cressley or Calderford to the pictures. If we went in decent time we could call for a drink afterwards and still have an early night.' She put her own squeeze on his arm. 'I expect you'd like an early night, wouldn't you?'

'If I say when we've had us dinners 'at I fancy a lie-down for an hour, you won't start arguin' with me, will you?'

'Not if that's what you want.' A silence. She said, 'I can allus find a job to do while I'm waiting for you.'

She felt his sideways look and knew it for a second to be uncertain, wondering. He could never, even now, be sure that she had that same need of him. Then it was a pleasure to feel with what ungrudging ease her face relaxed for him into a grin. It had, after all, been a long time for her as well.

3

'I hope,' she said, 'there's nobody going without a parachute for the sake of my cami-knickers.' She was holding up the square of material, feeling its weight and texture, having first thoughts about how she might cut into it.

Walter laughed. 'There's nobody jumping out of a plane without one, any road.' He was taking off his clothes in the curtain-filtered light of the bedroom. The door was firmly closed, the bolt home. Ella had washed up. She was the youngest of her family and the last

21

child living at home. Her father had gone out to potter in the garden and her mother, with a rug round her legs, was nodding in a chair which Walter had carried out for her on to the flags. 'That come out of a lot bigger piece,' he said. 'They get torn. T'chap 'at last used that could have landed in a tree for all I know.'

Ella peered closely at a stain in one corner. She took it to the window and lifted an edge of curtain.

'Hang on,' Walter said, 'I'm half-naked.'

'It couldn't be blood, could it?'

''Course it couldn't. Soak it. It'll come out.' He was beside her, his hands re-establishing their familiarity. 'Put it away and get undressed.'

'You lie down,' Ella said. 'I shan't be a minute.'

He stepped out of the heavy blue trousers and slipped off his underpants, adding them to the neat pile on a chair. Ella glanced sideways at him as she slid her frock off her shoulders. She would not have been caught staring but she did like seeing Walter naked. She had thought ever since the first time she had seen him totally so, across the width of this room, when he was not in any way flaunting himself but preoccupied with something happening outside, how natural and right was everything that was usually hidden by his clothes; how, in fact, their lack gave the often gawky man a new dimension of grace.

She felt an impulse to reach out and touch him, to make the first move and so let him know. But she was checked by an instinct that labelled it brazen just long enough for the moment to be lost. For Walter had turned to her and was offering hands that helped and fondled and finally hindered. When she spoke, laughing, he stood back and let her finish. But he would not leave her. He waited for the moment when she would have stepped round him to the bed, then drew her to him again.

There was no pretending she was cold: the sun had been in this room most of the morning and warmth had gathered under the low ceiling. Her nipples rose to

22

the touch of her hands on his naked back. He was not much taller than she was and she felt his flesh stir against her belly. She eased her hand between them and lightly encouraged the fleshy roll of foreskin as it drew down the hardening shaft and tightened into a stretched sheen of skin which made him gasp and sag at the waist as her already moist fingertips claimed its full length. He was always huge when he had been away from her for some time and she was tentative in awareness of the danger of bringing him before she could ensure satisfaction for herself. He would, in any case, be too quick for her now. But that over, and the abstinence of weeks behind them, she could promise herself with some certainty the easier drawn-out satisfaction of the night.

When he had lain down she crouched on the edge of the bed with her back to him and pushed the pessary as far into herself as she could.

'What are you doing?' She swung round and lay on her back, her knees drawn up. 'Do you have to?'

'Does it make any difference to you?'

'Well, no.'

'It would if I got pregnant.'

'I can't see 'at them things are much good anyway.'

'Safer than nothing. I'll take that much of a chance.'

'You do want a family, don't you?'

'Yes, I do. All in good time.'

He was silent, appearing to think about it. But when he said in a moment, 'I can't wait, love,' she knew that he spoke not of their children-to-be but of his present need as she eased further down the bed, drew him over on to her and felt the sweet stretch of his penetration.

His climax was gathering even then and she held him as, touching her with his gasped apology, he drove to an astonishing depth and emptied himself there.

Ella held him until she felt his insensible weight. She eased him over. She reached down for the towel she had provided herself with and tucked it up between her legs, pulling up the eiderdown to cover both of them just before Walter, his arm around her so that her head

23

rested on his shoulder, fell sound asleep on his back. She dozed a little herself then, her arm across his flat belly. Once she woke to find the edge of her hand against the damp, only scantily occupied sleeve of his penis, and she smiled. It was always a wonder to her that its might had ever been, that it could be aroused again in only a short time. Where had all that rampant power gone? She had it. It was with her. She had relieved him of what it expressed: his man's violent need, five weeks of waiting and – she fervently hoped – all the tensions of the day.

He twitched once or twice, his body jumping, just before he woke. In the moment of realizing where he was he tightened his hold on her and his free hand took the weight of her breast as she lay half on her side against him.

'Were you dreaming?'

'Hmm.'

'What about?'

'I was flying.' He was quiet. 'I often dream about that.'

She waited. Then, 'Walter . . . You're not still, well, pining for all that, are you?'

'No, no. No. I've written all that off. I'm best off as I am.' He shifted his hand and gently fondled. 'No, love, I wouldn't be surprised if you and me . . .'

'What, Walter?'

'Well, if we didn't have quite a cushy little war.'

Two

1

One evening in the following week, Ella was helping her sister-in-law, Winnie, to paper the living-room in the ramshackle cottage where Winnie had lived with Ella's brother and where she lived on her own now with her two small children. They had got the tricky bits on round the window before Winnie put up the blackout and lit the gas, and now, with one straight length after another, were making rapid strides towards the finish.

'How d'you like it now it's on?' Winnie asked, having asked the same question before in slightly different words, and Ella felt irritation move in her at her sister-in-law's seeming insistence on narrowing her non-committal 'very nice' into something more specific. She had known by the time they hung the second full length of paper that this was going to be a long way from the best decorating job she had ever been involved in. She didn't like Winnie's choice of wallpaper for a start, but that wouldn't have mattered had it not been cheap and flimsy, showing every bump and indentation in the walls. The flour-paste that Winnie had assured her she could mix herself was thick and lumpy; it soaked straight through the thin paper, making big damp patches which Ella doubted would ever disappear without a mark. Then there was the rising damp, to a height of a couple of feet in several places round the walls. They should have put on a tar-paper first to hold that back. But they hadn't. What pleasure was there in trying to make such a place look nice? Winnie herself had asked earlier, railing against the neglect of her landlord, who seemed quite happy to let the house fall down for want

25

of basic repairs. But what use was there ever, any-where, Ella thought, in doing only half a job? Still, Winnie seemed pleased enough as she stood away and surveyed their handiwork; as though, Ella thought, she had no idea, as though she simply couldn't see that it wasn't right, that it never would be right, and they might as well have spent their time on something else. I hate it, Ella thought, I wish I wasn't here. I wish I'd never offered. But how could she have got out of it, close as she had become to Winnie? Close? She sometimes felt that she had only two responses to her: she either felt sorry for her or she couldn't abide her. Mostly, these feelings were mixed. Just now pity was very much the loser and Ella fought to bring it back into the balance.

'I knew I was right to ask you,' Winnie was saying.

Ella didn't in fact know who else Winnie would have cared to ask. Ella's mother was a dab hand at papering. When she and Ronald's wife did a room together they worked with the rapid ease of professionals. Florrie could do it, too. Winnie was not popular with the family, though. She had never fitted into the ranks of the women-folk. She was a slut. She let them all down. But she had opened her heart to Ella after Thomas's death and Ella, touched by her candour and the appeal it contained, had felt impelled to help her through a sad time for both of them.

They stopped, had a minute. Winnie lit a cigarette.

'Shall we have enough paste here?'

'Oh, aye.'

The gaslight wavered. There was a hole in the mantle.

'I've had the paper ages,' Winnie said. 'Long before it got scarce. We were going to go right through the house. Smarten it all up. But it was like a lot of other things: we never got round to it.'

Ella had folded a dry cloth into a pad. She moved about, smoothing out wrinkles as she saw them in another angle of light. She had come to feel that every effort was a waste.

'Your Thomas used to reckon he could paper as well as any decorator he'd ever seen,' Winnie said. 'He was just never in a hurry to prove it.'

'Thomas liked to think most other people in this world got their money for nowt,' Ella said. 'I don't know if it's general among colliers, but our Ronald and Wilson are just the same. You try to get 'em to do a job, though. You heard about Florrie's bathroom, didn't you?'

'They haven't got a bathroom,' Winnie said.

'That's just it,' Ella said. 'She set her heart on one. What she really set her heart on was one of them new semis on Lowfield Lane, and they've got bathrooms built in. She got Wilson as far as looking at a partly finished one, but then he balked. He said it might be all right now, but what if he fell out of work again and couldn't keep up the payments. This was eighteen months afore t'war started.'

'Four hundred and fifty, weren't they?' Winnie said.

'I believe so.'

'I quite like that house Wilson and Florrie live in now.'

'It's all right,' Ella said. 'And Florrie said it was big enough to take a bathroom and still leave room for them and their three bairns. So when was Wilson going to tackle the landlord?'

'Landlords . . .' Winnie began.

'Well, to cut a long story short,' Ella said, before Winnie could get going on that subject again, 'Florrie asked him herself. Or at least, she sent a message by the rent collector, and he said no. He said he had no objection if they did it themselves, providing he approved the plans first; but he wouldn't do it for them.'

'Mingy sods, they are,' Winnie said. 'All of 'em. Your mam an' dad don't pay rent, do they?'

'Oh, no. It's theirs. Came to me dad through an aunt, or somebody. I've never enquired right into it.'

'What are you an' Walter going to do when you want a place of your own?'

'I don't know yet. Anyway, I was telling you. Wilson

said he wasn't going to pay for improvements to somebody else's property and Florrie told him he was cutting off his nose to spite his face. He ought to think about her and the kiddies, because *he* could get bathed at the pit.'

'Didn't it make a difference when they got pit-head baths and they weren't trailing all their muck home?' Winnie put in.

'Oh, aye. *I* can remember – just for a while – when me dad, our Wilson and our Thomas *all* came in black bright and stinkin' of pit-muck. They took turns in t'sink corner while me mam went on boiling water. Then Wilson got wed, me dad finished working, and for a while there was just Thomas.'

'Then he met me,' Winnie murmured, as though to herself. She docked her fag and put the unsmoked half on the mantelshelf.

'So Florrie got a plumber herself,' Ella said, determined to finish her story. 'She got a price and put it to Wilson. It was for partitioning their Catherine's bedroom and fitting a bath, a lav and a pedestal washbasin.

'They didn't need to go to all that expense and trouble, Wilson said. All it needed was a bath to stand in one corner of Catherine's room, and a board and a cloth they could cover it with when it wasn't in use. He could do all that his-self, he made out.

'Not long after that a couple of fellers come to Florrie's door with a bath on a wagon. Where does she want it? they ask her. It turns out 'at Wilson spotted it as he passed a demolition, agreed a price with the man in charge, and bought it.'

'But you need a back boiler an' all, and an extra tank in your loft,' Winnie said, showing, surprisingly, that she had been paying attention.

'O' course you do,' Ella said. 'And while Wilson's working all this out the bath stands in the yard outside their back door and Florrie says no more.

'It stands there for nigh on twelve month, until one day Florrie fills it full of soil, puts some stones and plants in and makes herself a rock garden.'

'Oh, of course, I've seen that,' Winnie said.

'I thought you would have. But never mention it when you're in their house, Winnie. Florrie reckons it was a fortnight before Wilson even noticed, and they've never talked about it from that day to this.'

Ella was laughing. She felt better, her irritability gone, for the present at least.

'I just put t'enamel bowl on t'floor and stand in that,' Winnie said after a time. 'The bairns are still little enough to stand in the sink.' She cocked her head at the door to the scullery behind her, with a shallow, oblong stone sink big enough, in fact, for a small child to sit in. 'Thomas got bathed at the pit,' she added unnecessarily.

For two or three years Thomas, Wilson, Ronald, and Ronald's lads, James and Arthur, had all worked at the same pit. But Thomas had been the only one of them below ground when disaster struck. He had remained there for seven weeks, with nine workmates. All killed by the blast, reported rescue workers who had seen them before the second blast had locked them away, sealed off by massive rockfalls and shifts in the strata. They would have been there still, many people claimed, had it been left to the coal-owners, and had the union president not raised hell and demanded they be got out no matter what the cost. Hardly a mark on most of them, the townspeople had heard after the bodies had been laid out in a room in the town hall and relatives had gone through the ordeal of identifying them.

Winnie had seemed easier in herself since then. There were small signs that she was taking more care, of herself, of her children, of the house; though with the house she fought a losing battle. The sag in the roof was plain to see as you approached along the lane. The paint had peeled, in places to the bare wood. Putty and cement had fallen out round the windows. Winnie had plugged with rags the worst of the cracks, and stuffed sacks in the gap under the door where in bad weather the wind whistled and rain ran in.

Tonight was fine, though. There was moonlight. The

29

cottage stood a hundred yards from the road. The only sound in the stillness was the hiss of gas in the broken mantle. When Winnie's hip jarred the trestle table she was pasting on, the screech of its feet on the flagstone floor made Ella, who had half-turned away, start visibly.

'We've nearly finished.'

'Do you want a cup of tea?'

'No, let's knock on.' She held up the last roll. 'Linda and Brian are quiet. I was sure one of 'em would have been down nosey-poking.'

'Oh, I made certain they'd sleep tonight.'

'How did you do that?'

'Gave 'em something.'

'You could put it on t'market.'

'It is on t'market.' Winnie opened a cupboard and took out a small flat bottle. She held it so that Ella could see the label. 'I gave 'em a drop of this.'

'Cough mixture?' Ella said. 'They haven't got colds, have they?'

'Oh, Ella, you are green sometimes.'

'Me? Green?'

'They don't mind the taste, and a little drop sends 'em off in no time.' When Ella did not respond, Winnie said, 'I know a woman what gets through three bottles a week.'

'Not for her kiddies.'

'For herself.' She took in Ella's expression. 'Don't think I give it 'em every night.'

'I should think not. And I hope you don't take it yourself.' Ella felt faintly apprehensive at this new example of Winnie's offhand ways.

'I've tried it but it does nowt for me. No, I get my nirvana out of a gin bottle. T'only trouble is, it takes more an' more all the time.' She glanced at Ella as she put the bottle away. A faint sardonic smile touched her lips. 'There's one big thing stands between me an' drinkin' all I might.'

'What's that?'

'Poverty,' Winnie said.

30

'How d'you think your mam an' dad 'ud take it if you started with a kid?' Winnie asked all at once, when they had begun working again.

'How d'you mean?'

'I mean it strikes me they're all right with little 'uns as long as they're only visiting.'

'We'd have to look out for somewhere,' Ella said.

'Would Walter want to buy?'

'On RAF pay? Talk sense, Winnie.'

'Thomas was talking about buying, just before he was killed,' Winnie said. 'That's what makes all this so maddening. We might have been out of it by now.'

Ella suspected that Winnie had only thought of this since she had told her about Wilson and Florrie looking at new houses. She had begun to catch Winnie making things up. The basis of it seemed to be a desire to gloss over the shortcomings of her marriage. It looked better to her now than it had while Thomas was alive.

Ella's brother had beaten his wife and Ella sometimes wondered whether he had known he would end up knocking her about when he went back time after time to that lonely farm where he had found her and where she kept ready for him her open arms and legs. The way Winnie told it she had been aware of the risk she took: that Thomas would come for that and nothing else and never come again when he had tired of it. But he had apparently not tired of it until it was available to him every night in his own bed. Perhaps he had come to despise himself for it then and to use her slovenly ways as an excuse to take it out on her, so that she became even less capable of pride in herself, and he more deeply embittered; each bringing out the worst in the other.

They hung the last few lengths of wallpaper working steadily and not talking. They had found a rhythm now that the job was done. Ella wiped her hands and looked round at Winnie.

'Give that table-top a wipe over, Winnie, before it dries sticky.'

'There's no point in keeping this bit of paste, is there?'

'No. You can be putting the kettle on now, if you like. I'll swill the bucket and put the remains down the drain.'

Outside, Ella could see nearly as far as the road. She detected a movement and stood for a moment with the empty bucket in her hand. 'It's like daylight out there,' she told Winnie when she went back in.

'I expect somebody'll be catching it.'

'They'll not waste a night like this.'

The war had entered a new phase. London had been bombed every night since early September. They saw pictures in cinema newsreels of flames in the darkness, of firemen on swaying extension ladders pouring water endlessly into burning buildings with no apparent effect. They marvelled that anything still stood, that people managed somehow to live among it all; and they were glad that they did not live in a city themselves.

They had folded the trestle-table and carried it into the scullery when Winnie cocked her head at footsteps outside.

'There's somebody walkin' round the house.'

'I thought I saw somebody up the lane,' Ella told her.

A firm knock on the door made them both jump.

'Are you going to answer it?' Ella said, aware that her voice was little more than a whisper.

'Seein' as you're here, I will,' Winnie said. 'I wouldn't otherwise.'

The knock came again. Winnie went and stood with her head close to the door.

'Who is it?'

A man's voice said something that Ella couldn't catch.

'Who did you say?'

Again the man's voice.

Winnie said, 'I don't believe it,' but she was looking

round and speaking to Ella now. Her colour had risen in only a moment. A funny smile came to her face. 'Well . . .' She stood for a few more seconds before opening the door and peering out. 'You'd better come in before t'bobby catches you.'

She shut the door quickly after the man who stepped in past her. He was not tall but he gave an immediate impression of coiled wiry strength. His face had a natural high colour and he had, Ella noticed as he moved nearer the central gaslight, the longest and most lustrously dark eyelashes she had ever seen on a man. He was dressed in a well worn tweed jacket of the countryman's kind that could contain all manner of mysteries, dead and alive, and cord trousers. All this Ella took in before he stopped in the middle of the floor and doffed his cap, to show a round nut of a head with very short, soft dark hair. His dark eyes flickered on to her as he nodded.

'Evenin', missus.'

Winnie's eyes were on him as she said to Ella, 'You heard me mention Mole Templeton, from the farm.'

'Oh, yes . . .'

'This is him.'

'Alwyn, me mother called me,' the man said. 'Everybody else calls me Mole.'

'This is me sister-in-law, Mrs Lindley.'

'Pleased to meet you.' Templeton stuck out his hand. It was hard and calloused but didn't abuse its strength.

'I've just made a pot of tea. Would you like some?'

'Be very welcome.' He looked round awkwardly.

'Get one of them chairs,' Winnie said. 'We've just been wallpapering.'

'Very nice,' Mole said.

Ella watched him as he moved the straight chair, then placed another one for her. She could not take her eyes off him.

'You're a long way from home, Mole, aren't you?' Winnie said. She handed him a mug and spooned sugar into it. 'See, I haven't forgotten how many you like. Or

33

used to.' She looked at him as he nodded thanks and took a first sip. 'What brings you to these parts?'

'I came to see you.'

'Did you, now?'

'I heard about your trouble.'

'Bad news travels a long way.' Winnie found the half-smoked cigarette that she had put aside earlier. 'Don't you think it's a funny time of night to come visiting a woman on her own?'

'You took some finding.'

'Have you been asking about the village for me?'

'It was either that or go away without seeing you.'

'Hmm. You mean you heard I'd lost me husband and you upped and came all that way just to see me?'

'Old friends can be a help.'

'Oh, aye,' Winnie said.

Ella wanted to tell her not to be so hard and ungrateful. But she also knew that from the moment he had entered the house Mole had aroused in her, too, a woman's wariness.

His hand dipped into a pocket. It came out holding a flat half-bottle of whisky. He showed it to Winnie with a questioning lift of his eyebrows.

'Go on, then,' Winnie said. 'Why not?' She held out her mug.

Templeton turned to Ella. 'Missus?'

'Er, no, I don't think so, thanks. It's summat I've never got the taste for.'

Templeton took his neat, from the bottle. He wiped the neck of the bottle with the palm of his hand and put the bottle away.

'So,' Winnie said, 'how's everything at the farm?'

'I'm running things now.'

'Oh, are you?' Winnie flicked an old-fashioned look at Ella.

'The gaffer's dead,' Templeton said. 'Last year. Collapsed at market. Mrs Atkinson relies on me now.'

'If you're all she's got she will do,' Winnie said.

'A big do, wasn't it, that you lost your husband in?'

Templeton said after a silence. 'I saw it in a paper first.'

'Aye. He'd changed shifts, y'know. He wasn't on his reg'lar job at all.'

Ella watched her carefully while, as if compelled, Winnie told him the detail, the circumstances she had blamed herself for. But she remained in control.

'They did get 'em out, then?'

'Eventually.'

Templeton nodded. 'Well, you'll feel the better for that.'

Winnie lifted her head. Her voice changed. 'I've got a couple of kids, y'know.'

'I heard that as well,' Templeton said. 'I thought about you when that ship went down.'

'The *Empress of Britain*?'

'Aye. Terrible thing.'

Carrying children to the safety of Canada, the liner had been torpedoed and sunk in the North Atlantic.

'Folk 'at can do a thing like that . . .' Templeton shook his head. 'They're not fit to live the'selves. They should be put down like vermin.' He looked round at Ella. 'Don't you think so, Missus?'

'Oh, yes.' It had become the stuff of many a nightmare.

They were all silent. Then Winnie said, as if it were merely keeping the conversation going, 'How is it you've not been called up yourself?'

'Wouldn't have me.' He tapped the side of his face. 'Perforated eardrum. Allus was a bit hard of hearin', if you remember.'

'I never knew you to miss owt important.'

Winnie contemplated him. He did not seem to mind. He drank his tea and looked at the small fire of slack which smoked without flame in the grate, until Winnie said, 'Have some more tea. Pour him another cup, Ella, and have one yourself, while I pop out to the back.'

Ella lifted the teapot, offering it to Templeton.

'Ta. Is your husband down the pit?'

'No, he's a butcher by trade, but he's in the RAF now.'

35

'A long way off?'

'Not that far. He gets home.'

'That's not so bad, then, eh?'

'No.'

She said in a moment, 'Won't you have missed your last bus home?'

He shrugged. He cocked his head at the door through which Winnie had left the room.

'We were courtin', y'know. Afore your brother came along.'

Ella had not known. It was not the way Winnie had told it to her.

'Were they all right together?'

She noticed now the way he turned his head full-face towards her, as though he wanted to look over her further shoulder, but in reality to bring his good ear into range of her voice. She lifted her voice slightly.

'They had their barneys, like all married couples.' She added, 'She's a bonny couple of kiddies.'

Templeton nodded without speaking. From his top pocket he took a short-stemmed pipe; from elsewhere a tobacco tin worn to a shine with use. He pressed coarse tobacco into the bowl of the pipe and lit it with a match.

As soon as she had refilled his cup Ella had returned to her chair, where she was not directly facing him. She was watching him, taking in again his boots, his cord trousers, the capacious jacket that, she noted now, was a little too long in the sleeves, the crimson neckerchief inside the collarless shirt, the weathered red of his neck above it, the high bone of his cheek, brought out now as he sat with his face slightly turned from her; and, most of all, the startling luxuriance of those lashes.

She had begun to wonder what was keeping Winnie when the back door opened and shut and water ran into the scullery sink. Winnie came into the room wiping her hands on her pinafore and said at once, as though Ella had transmitted her own thought, 'You'll surely never get a bus back up there at this time.'

'I made me mind up,' Templeton said. 'I wasn't going away till I'd found you.'

'I see.'

'It's a bigger place than I thought.'

'Little enough for word to get about.'

'I said I was an old friend.'

'Not much else you could say, I suppose.'

Ella said, 'Does anybody know what time it is?'

'You're not going yet, are you, Ella?'

'I've got to work in the morning.'

'You'll be late,' Winnie said to Mole. 'You'll be able to walk straight in and get started.'

'She owes me a couple of days,' Templeton said.

'You mean she doesn't expect you back?' Winnie looked at Ella over his head. 'What are we going to do with you, then? Do you fancy walkin' twenty-five mile and sleepin' in a hedge-bottom?'

'I'll manage.'

Ella was getting up a little hesitantly from her chair, feeling somehow that she ought not to leave this minute, but not seeing either just what part she was expected to play if she stayed, when Templeton said, 'I didn't come empty handed,' and plunged his hand deep into a low pocket on the other side of his jacket; deep inside, out of sight.

'That's a nice one,' Winnie said as they saw the rabbit. Its head lolled.

'You know what to do with it?'

''Course I do. When was it killed?'

'Yesterday.'

Ella was sure that Winnie was capable of skinning the rabbit but not equally certain that she wouldn't spoil it in the cooking.

'I'm sorry I haven't one for you, Missus.'

'That's all right, thanks all the same. We're not going short, so far.'

Templeton stood up. Winnie said, 'Where are you going?'

'Is it . . . ?'

'Oh, out the back. I'll show you.'

She went out with him. She took the rabbit and came back without it. She said, 'I told you about him. Remember? How he weighed Thomas up.'

'Yes. I've thought since that you wondered if they might get to blows.'

'If I'd known how handy Thomas was with his fists I might have worried a bit more.'

'He just told me 'at you were courtin' before Thomas turned up.'

'The lying devil.'

'He must wish it had been so.'

'Well, it wasn't.'

'Happen he thought it over after you'd gone and was sorry he'd missed his chance.'

'You an' your imagination.'

'Look how far he's come to see you.'

'Aye, and look how he finds me. Just look at this dump. And me.'

Winnie plucked at her pinafore and looked down at the laceless pumps on her feet. But at least, Ella thought, her hair looked as if it had had a comb through it today. And that was an improvement on what had been.

'I don't suppose you were allus got up for a garden party when you worked on the farm.'

'No, but do you think Thomas would have trailed back all that way if I'd looked like I do now?' Winnie put a hand to her face. 'God, Ella, but I have let meself go. I've come to a pretty pass, and I just can't seem to help it.'

'Come on, Winnie,' Ella said. 'It's not that bad. I've thought once or twice lately 'at you were, well, coming round, having a try . . .'

'I know. I know what you mean. An' then I think, what's the use?'

'It's pride, y'know, Winnie,' Ella said gently. 'It's self-respect 'at'll save you. There's nowt else.'

Winnie found a hanky and blew her nose.

'You don't think he's sloped off, do you, without saying goodbye?'

'He'll be giving us time to talk about him,' Ella said. 'He's not as simple as he looks, that one.'

'How can I turn him out to walk all that way?' Winnie asked.

'How can you let him stop here with you on your own?'

'You mean folk'll talk.'

'If he's seen leaving here tomorrow morning they'll talk. Besides which . . .' she added in a moment.

'He could stretch out on there.' Winnie pointed to the old sagging sofa pushed to the back of the room.

'I thought you once told me he was allus trying to get you on your own?'

'Oh, a handful of owt he could grab when he got near enough,' Winnie said. 'He won't try to *rape* me, y'know.'

'I don't know. It's what *you* know 'at matters.'

'I know I can't turn him out.'

'It's up to you.'

'Oh, Ella, don't be like that. Don't be like all the rest of your bloody family.'

'I'm not being like that. I'm only warning you. Your name'll be mud if anybody sees him.'

'Bugger me name,' Winnie said, and Ella could see now that she had firmly made up her mind. 'What do I care what *they* all think? They'll think what they want whatever I do. They've never cared bloody tuppence for me, so why should I care about what they think now?'

3

Ella walked along the lane in the white moonlight. She was surprised that there had been no air-raid warning yet tonight, no enemy planes passing overhead to their targets in Manchester and Liverpool. There was still time for them to come later, when everyone had got off to sleep. She and her mother had got up and gone into the cellar a couple of times; now they followed Ella's father's example and took no notice, aware that if a bomb did fall in the immediate vicinity it would be accidental. The prime targets were elsewhere.

Mole Templeton had shown no surprise when Winnie told him he could stay till morning. 'I *can't* turn him out, Ella,' Winnie had said, 'and that's the end of it.' As for talk, Ella knew that, recently widowed as she was, Winnie would have been talked about if seen on the street with Mole, let alone for entertaining him as a lodger. She herself remembered how her flesh had crawled in anticipation of it when she had wanted to see Howard Strickland while Walter was in Canada. In this small, tight-knit town even dark alleys and back doors were not always enough to hide secrets. A man had one pint too many . . . Two women exchanged the time of day and one wanted to score by proving how much she knew . . .

Ella started and threw up her hands as a man vaulted a wall and dropped into the lane in front of her. She didn't know what to do. She stood where she had stopped, aware how clearly she was signalling her apprehension. Then the man spoke.

'Is that you, Auntie Ella?'

She felt her muscles relax. It was her nephew, Arthur Palmer.

'What the hummer are you doing, frightening folk like that, Arthur?'

'I'm sorry. I was cuttin' the corner. I didn't know there was anybody about.'

As they moved closer to each other they lowered their voices in the quiet. He was just turned twenty. His older brother, James, Ella's own age, employed the 'auntie' with heavy-handed humour, but Arthur, only three years younger, used it from habit, without self-consciousness, it seeming natural to his earnest good-nature and a way of showing his respect.

'Where are you off to, anyway?'

40

'Up to see me Auntie Winnie. She's a job she wants me to do.'

'At this time o' night?'

'I've been workin'. I'm on afternoons.'

'All t'same . . .'

'If I see what she wants I can take me tackle t'next time. She never goes to bed early, does she?'

'She was going when I left, though,' Ella said, and thought, Now I've told a lie for her, whether she wanted it or not. She said, 'We've been papering.'

'Well, I might just as well call in, now I'm here.'

'You'd be best off walking me home. You just gave me a fright.'

Arthur looked along the lane to the house.

'I did promise.'

Ella took his arm, just above the elbow.

'Come away, Arthur. Come another time, in daylight.'

He let himself be led a few steps. He was a gentle boy, easy to tease, quick to be embarrassed. But he could be stubborn. He said, 'Is there summat amiss?'

'I was just thinking about gossip.'

'What gossip?'

'A woman on her own being visited at this time of night.'

'She's me auntie.'

'In-law,' Ella said.

'If she doesn't mind why should anybody else?'

He had taken his arm from her hold and come to a stop again.

'She's got company, Arthur.'

'I could just pop in and have a word.'

Ella sighed.

'It's somebody she knew from before she was married. Come to look her up.'

'A chap, d'you mean?'

'Yes.'

'How long d'you reckon he'll be stoppin'?'

'There's nowt in it but he's missed his bus and she's letting him stay the night.'

41

'Oh.'

'There's nowt in it,' Ella said again. 'It's just out of the kindness of her heart.'

'Oh.'

'So you see . . .'

'She's not ready for bed yet, then, is she?'

'No, I expect they'll sit up till all hours, talkin' about old times. Only, you don't want to go bargin' in now, do you?'

'No.'

After another long look at the dark shape of the cottage, he walked slowly with Ella towards the mouth of the lane.

'I told her,' Ella said, 'what folk 'ud say if he was spotted leavin'. But she'd taken pity on him and I couldn't budge her. So I'm telling you now, whatever you do don't let it slip.'

'I'm not daft,' he said, and there was something so savage in his tone that Ella was taken by surprise.

'I wouldn't have told you if I hadn't had to.'

'I'm sorry t'penny didn't drop.'

'There's nothing in it, Arthur.'

'You don't have to tell me. I shan't go blabbin' it about.'

Ella couldn't quite make him out. She said with gentle banter, 'Of course you won't. You're a big lad now.'

'And don't you start that,' Arthur said. 'Don't you get like the others. They seem to think I'm nobbut just out of short pants. As if I'm not a man, doing a man's job.'

Ella waited, wondering not so much at what Arthur had said, but at the intensity of his resentment. The joke, as far as he was concerned, was over.

'And if you think I can't keep me mouth shut,' he went on after a breath, 'I'll tell you this – I kept it shut when I'd seen you down town with that Mr Strickland.' Ella froze. 'And I knew who he was. I remembered him from when he come and lodged with me grandma. Him and that older chap.'

'Mr Keighley,' Ella murmured.

'Aye, Mr Keighley. And I'm not sayin' there was owt

in *that*,' Arthur said. 'Except that you seemed to want to go round corners about it.'

'It's a long story,' Ella said.

'And your own business. So I said nowt.'

'It's hard to explain,' Ella began and Arthur broke in on her.

'I don't want to know. But I'm not as green as I'm cabbage-lookin', that's all I want to tell you.'

Three

1

Ella let herself into the house as the Masons Arms turned out. A man said good night to her and she responded. Only recently had she acquired her own key, when she persuaded her parents to have a Yale lock fitted, and she enjoyed the freedom it gave her to come in when she liked without the thought that she was keeping one of them up. There was a time when they would have gone to bed and left the door unlocked; but one morning Sugden had found evidence of someone's having been in their outside w.c. late at night, and this with the unsettling effect of the blackout had undermined the easy confidence of pre-war days.

The gaslight was turned to its dimmest and she adjusted that before taking off her coat and sitting in the rocking-chair. The fire was banked-up and she left it undisturbed. She would go to bed before long but this was the quiet hour, the only time in the day when she could be alone and think things over.

Her parents' cottage resembled Winnie's. They had been built about the same time and could have been variations by the same hand. The most important difference between them, though, was that when you walked into this house you knew you were in a real home; and that came not from fancy furnishings, which a family of nine children had never run to, but from the sense of a working household, of washing and cleaning and baking; where a job to be done had never been sacrificed to hopeless, idle lounging by the fireside.

There were some magazines on the table, which made Ella wonder if her sister, Ada, had been. It was Ada

44

who brought this kind of glossy publication, passed on by her employer, when she had read them herself; though her visits were fewer now that petrol was scarce.

Ella opened a copy of *Good Housekeeping*. There was a piece on how to feed five on three pounds, ten shillings a week – a family of four and a maid. She sometimes wondered who such things were written for; or whether she had any business reading them. Here too was an article by Daphne du Maurier about writing letters in wartime, telling you to be cheerful and keep your trials and tribulations to yourself, not pass them on to the men in the forces, who had enough to worry about. Sensible enough. But there was a little sketch of peacetime letter-writing, with the envelopes left on a salver in the hall for the parlour-maid to take out. Ella thought she might have identified with that – if they had had a salver, and a hall to leave it in; and had she not realized all too certainly that in that scene *she* was the parlour-maid. Only someone like Ada could manage to be parlour-maid, cook and chauffeur's wife and put on the airs and graces of those who paid her wages.

Ella went quietly up the stairs. From the bottom of her wardrobe she took the shoe-box in which she kept her papers: old greetings cards, a photograph or two, newspaper reports of births, marriages, deaths; her birth and marriage certificates, and her letters. Walter's letters written from Canada were in there. To them, only that week, she had added her first letter from Howard Strickland.

She took the box downstairs. Of course she had insisted on telling Arthur about Howard. Something about him, anyway. She had told him how he had come with their twice-yearly lodger, Mr Keighley, because he was to take over Mr Keighley's customers in the watches and clocks line; how he had been found guilty of stealing from the firm, and how the next time she had seen him was when he came as a soldier, stationed in the town after Dunkirk. He had wanted to explain, to tell her that he was innocent; but she had not felt able to

45

invite him home to do it because of her parents, who had liked and trusted Mr Keighley and would never have believed anything which contradicted what he said. In Mr Strickland's case they had taken Mr Keighley to be prosecuting counsel, judge and jury. So Ella had gone out with Olive Sims, who had been picked up by Howard's friend Tony, using her as a cover.

A garbled version, which left out the romance. Olive knew about the romance (and would have been compelled to make some up had there not been any), but nothing about Howard's short prison sentence. It hadn't seemed Ella's place to tell her; they weren't really friends and there was no need for it. But she had had to make some kind of explanation to Arthur other than confessing that she had thought herself in love with Howard, while her husband was serving his country in Canada. The way she had let Howard go and turned to Walter with a clear conscience, she owed herself a clean slate. So she had told Arthur what she had kept from Olive and consoled herself for the breach of self-imposed confidence by reflecting that it didn't really matter now what anybody in Daker thought of Howard Strickland since none of them would ever see him again.

But he had said he would write, and now he had done: 'We are still in England and can't be sure yet just where we are bound for. There is no shortage of rumour, as you may imagine; but if I repeated any of them it would no doubt be blue-pencilled, so I'll leave it at that.

'Apart from that there is nothing I can add to what I said, or tried to say when we last saw each other, the night before we left. You gave me then what little you could spare, or, I suppose, as much as you felt you had any right to give. I shall never forget that. More than your gentle embrace and your shy kisses I treasure the spiritual joy of that quiet hour and my memories of the peace of it will sustain me through whatever might lie ahead . . .'

I'm a married woman, Ella told herself, and he has no

right to say such things to me. But oh, she thought, how beautifully he says them!

'Please change your mind about writing to me. With all this terrible bombing it can't be assumed that anybody is safe, even on the Home Front, so an occasional word that will stop me worrying will be a great relief. Surely I can ask for that much? In the meantime I send this c/o your friend Olive, as arranged.'

Her 'friend' Olive, who, while a workmate, had never been a 'friend', had only become involved in Ella's business because she happened to be there when Howard Strickland suddenly appeared again. Olive had passed her the envelope with the one word 'Ella' written on it while they were at work. Ella had taken out the folded sheet and glanced at the signature before looking Olive in the eye and mouthing against the hum and rattle of the weaving shed, 'Why is it open?'

Olive screwed up her face. 'I'll tell you later.'

'You've no bloody business opening my private letters.'

'I'll explain,' Olive mouthed, and went out of sight, to her own job.

Still blazing mad, Ella had cornered her at dinnertime. Her thoughts had run on through the morning's work. From the moment she had realized that to see Howard again she would have to take Olive at least partly into her confidence, she had been afraid she would regret it. Olive, sexually inexperienced but sex-mad, open-eyed and loose-tongued, inquisitve but tactless, was about the last woman Ella would have chosen to share any secret. And now she had behaved so perfectly in character Ella had barely restrained herself from going for her in front of everybody.

She held up the envelope before Olive's face and pointed to what was written on it.

'Does that say "Olive"?'

'No.'

'Then what do you mean by opening it and reading it?'

Olive said, 'It was waiting when I got home from work last night. I opened it thinking it was from Tony,

47

and found that inside. There wa' nowt else. Then me mam came in. "Is that from your soldier-boy?" she asks me. "Have they gone overseas yet?" So I opened it so's I could reckon to tell her. I didn't read it properly, not every word. I mean, I didn't read it twice or owt like that. I just wanted to know. They haven't left England yet, have they?'

'They hadn't when this was written, any road.' Something that Olive had said made her ask, 'What did you mean when you said you thought it was from Tony?'

'There wa' my name and address on the other envelope – the one it came in.'

'Well, don't you know what Tony's handwriting looks like?'

Olive shook her head. 'No.' Something began to give way in her face. 'I've never heard from him. He hasn't written.'

Ella had an idea that something a bit more intimate than a cuddle and some 'shy kisses' had taken place between Olive and Tony. As tears suddenly welled up in the other girl's eyes, Ella shifted her stance so that Olive was shielded from the one or two women glancing their way. There were still some who could not understand how Ella Palmer and Olive Sims had become so thick with each other.

'I mean,' Olive managed through her tears, 'Howard's only chasing rainbows, isn't he? But Tony ought to know how I feel.'

The shoe-box was on the table beside Ella. She replaced Howard's letter and rocked herself. She ought to go to bed: she had to be up early in the morning. But she let her thoughts drift. Poor Olive, wondering whether she had sold herself cheap to a man whom she hardly knew; a man who would soon be God knew where, to be seen again God only knew when. If ever. And hearing from Howard had served to resurrect the questions Ella had thought she had stopped asking on the night she had seen him last, the night that Walter had come home without warning and she had taken

48

him to her in a way that seemed to her to signify once and for all the putting away from her of one man and the binding to her for ever of the other.

2

The air-raid siren startled her. It always did. It was like nothing that any of them had heard before. It reared itself out of silence until its colossal rising and falling moan filled all the air. None but the stone-deaf and the dead could sleep through that. When it had wound itself down again into memory that could never quite retain its awesome power, Ella heard a floorboard give overhead. As a stair creaked she got up and broke open the fire. She was setting a kettle to boil on the coals when the chamber door opened and her mother came in.

'Now . . .'

'Now then . . .'

Patience, in her flannel nightgown, had thrown an openknit wool shawl over her shoulders.

'Are you going to be warm enough like that?'

'I shall be when t'fire burns through. You're still dressed. Have you only just come in?'

'I've been in a while. I was just coming to bed. Is me dad stopping where he is?'

'You know what he is when he's made his mind up.'

'Yes, pig-headed.'

'Now, Ella, that's not your sort of talk. Not about your father, any road.'

'Stubborn, then.'

'At least you know where you are with him.'

'Aye, I'll say that,' Ella conceded. 'Are you thinking of going down the cellar?'

'No, I'm not.'

'Then I reckon me dad's as safe as we are. And tucked up snug for it.'

Her mother settled herself more comfortably into the

49

rocker. 'Give that fire another poke, Ella, and get that kettle boiling.'

Patience was sixty-six now. She had been running to heavy flesh at hips and waist but had recently shed some weight. The simple style of her iron-grey hair, cut short in the neck, emphasised the breadth of her face, with its habitual placid good-nature.

Heavy feet pounded by outside. One man, running. 'He's in a hurry.'

Ella checked the curtains at both windows for light-revealing chinks. Their air-raid warden was Mr Selby, the newsagent, who knew practically everybody. It didn't matter if you were a customer of his or not, if he saw a light he banged on your door and reprimanded you for it.

'Martha says our Ronald's joined t'Home Guard,' Patience remarked as they watched the kettle. Ronald was Ella's oldest brother. 'She says he's never at home.'

Ella said, 'Do they have their headquarters in t'pub?' and Patience allowed herself a faint smile, though Ronald's – and Thomas's – fondness for beer had caused her many a heartache.

Ella put tea into the pot and sat down again in her father's chair.

'Our Ada hasn't been, has she?'

'No. Why?'

Ella waved her hand at the table. 'Them books.'

'Oh, Martha brought them. I told you she'd called.'

'No, you didn't. You said she'd told you about our Ronald joining t'Home Guard.'

'When she called.'

How else could she have known? her tone implied, and Ella didn't pursue it further. She was used to the idiosyncracies of parents old enough to be her grandparents; who, in fact, had grandchildren her own age. Recently, and especially since her marriage and the status that had given her, she had had a feeling of gradually taking charge. While not so long ago she would have deferred in almost everything, she now found that hers was the opinion which often decided an issue.

She scalded the tea and got out cups and saucers and milk.

'She doesn't buy 'em, does she?' she asked, referring to her sister-in-law and the magazines.

'She got 'em from t'woman she cleans for.'

'Cleans for? She's never going out cleaning, is she?' It was the first Ella had heard of that.

'It's only two mornings a week,' Patience said. 'It's that woman on Bank View Road where Wilson's lass used to go for piano lessons. It's a sister what lives with 'em what gives lessons, an' it wa' through her 'at Florrie came to tell Martha 'at they were short of a bit of help. Florrie wouldn't go herself, what with her bairns still at school, and in any case she hasn't got same appetite for hard work 'at Martha has; so Martha said she'd help 'em out for a while. It's a bit of cash for her an' all.'

'Unless our Ronald docks it off her housekeepin',' Ella said.

'No, he's not as maungy as that, for all his faults.' Patience sighed appreciatively as Ella handed her her tea. 'Anyway, that's what she's doing.'

'I've seen our Arthur tonight,' Ella said conversationally, before she had stopped to consider.

'Where was he?'

Ella had asked Arthur to keep a secret and it struck her that his visiting Winnie at the hour she had seen him was a bit of information she would rather not pass on until she had thought a bit more about it.

'Oh, I just ran into him.'

'He's a nice lad, Arthur,' her mother said. 'A bit on the old-fashioned side. I don't know who he gets that from.' She smiled. 'Our James likes to plague him, but he can only go so far.'

Ella looked at the ceiling and lifted her hand as her sharper ears picked up the first sound in the sky above them.

'Listen . . .'

The unmistakable intermittent thrum of enemy aircraft

51

engines that they had all learned to identify grew louder as Patience turned her head.

'That's them all right.'

'Are they going or coming back?'

'Oh, they're going. They're on their way to Lancashire.'

The sound became fainter, then died.

'I'm going back to bed when I've drunk this,' Patience said. 'I'll have another cup, though.' Ella poured. 'Did you get done at Winnie's?'

'Oh, aye, for what it was worth.'

'Wasn't she satisfied?'

'Oh, she was. I didn't think it was up to much, though.'

'Well,' her mother said comfortably, 'if you've done your bit.'

They were on dangerous ground now. If Patience went on extracting information in that simple way she had – almost like setting traps – of asking one thing at a time and waiting for the answer, Ella might find herself telling outright lies to cover Mole Templeton's presence. Simply not mentioning it would make her nowhere near so uneasy. So she changed the subject.

'You say our Ronald's joined the Home Guard?'

'Aye. Martha says somebody told him 'at with his experience he'd very likely soon be a sergeant.'

Ronald had served in the last war. Ella had heard a rumour, though, that Hitler had said he would not recognize the Home Guard as real soldiers, but have them all shot when he invaded; which put a different complexion on blacking your face and crawling about in hedge bottoms, then retiring to the pub for a pint or two. Ella said nothing to her mother. Since Mr Churchill had broadcast to the nation at the beginning of September, talking about the Spanish Armada and Nelson and Napoleon, the threat of invasion had receded again, as it had after Dunkirk. It looked as if Hitler had missed his chance a second time. But who could be sure? And after the triumphs of the summer and the Battle of Britain there was not much left to crow about. Hanging on was the main thing now. Hang on while he throws

52

everything he's got at you. Not that it was all one-sided.
There had been some British bomber raids on Germany
too. It was when Ella thought of British lads sitting up
there in the searchlights and the anti-aircraft fire that
she blessed the day Walter had been found wanting, and
felt not the slightest degree of guilt in her gratitude.

In her silent drift into thought she had let go of the
reins of conversation. Patience took them.

'How do you find Winnie just lately?' She added before
Ella could reply, 'I have to ask because I don't see much
of her these days.'

'You could happen have a walk on and see her sometime.'

'Nay, t'door's open here.'

Ella hesitated. She wanted to put Winnie's point of
view without seeming to be critical herself.

'I think she feels out of things.'

'She'd feel more in things if she brought them bairns
to see their grandmother.' There was a silence. 'Has
anybody called her to her face?'

'Not to her face, no.'

'Then I don't know what she's got to complain about.'

'She doesn't complain,' Ella said.

'How do you come to know so much, then?'

'It's just a feeling I get.'

'Imagination.'

'Well, she doesn't come, does she? That's not imagination.'

'She's dozy.'

'Oh, aye.'

'What does she do with her bairns when there's an air-
raid warning?'

'Takes 'em down her cellar.'

'An' keeps herself warm with a bottle o' something,
I don't doubt.'

'I don't think she's doing as much drinking lately.'

'She can't afford it,' Patience said. 'Wait till she gets
her hands on t'compensation for Thomas, though.'

'I don't know,' Ella said. 'I've just had a feeling that

53

she was pulling herself together more since they got the men out of the pit.'

But her mother wasn't listening. She had taken the cue for one of her favourite ruminative homilies, on the evils of drink.

'I've known some terrible things, Ella lass. Men what'd take their wages into a pub on Friday night and not go home till they were penniless. Some 'at owed so much on t'slate their wages were mortgaged afore they got 'em. Others 'at used to see things. Crawling things. All sorts. I'd an uncle like that. They had to hold him down or he'd have done himself a damage. Everything sacrificed to it – food, home, all chance of a decent life. Some women couldn't stand it; they gave in and took to drink themselves. Can you blame 'em?'

But you do, Ella thought. Women, in her mother's view, should be made of sterner stuff. She found her another cup in the teapot as she went on talking, illustrating with a wealth of examples, all capable of shocking – and meant to – until she gave a sudden almost involuntary chuckle and related the leavening anecdote of Ella's Uncle Nathaniel, Patience's eldest brother, who had lain sound asleep under the living-room table all evening while his wife Lavinia did the rounds of all their nearby relatives in search of him, and all night while she lay in bed wondering whether the morning would dawn with the disgrace of his being brought home by the police.

'She got up about six o'clock to make a cup of tea,' Patience said. 'She dropped a spoon on t'floor, bent down an' spotted a pair o' working boots with feet in 'em under the table. There was Nat, curled up like a bairn, still fast on.' Patience chuckled again. 'I can laugh over him because he turned into one of the soberest men who ever walked shoe leather. A bit too much so, if the truth's told, 'cos it was when your Aunt Lavinia took to religion. I don't mean she started going to church more often. No, she got on preaching at little mission chapels and calling folk names. Spoilt your Uncle Nat in a way. He allus had a touch of mischief in him afore then.

Fond of a joke. Lavinia never could see a joke. Some funny matches . . .'

'People marry people 'at's there to be courted,' Ella said. She thought about herself and Walter. Only his persistence had won her over.

'They can go out o' t'district and not do any better,' Patience said. 'Look at our Thomas. Twenty-five mile he went. And went back again. And when he gets her what does he do with her? You can see more than I can if you can tell me what she had about her to make him trail all that way.'

Or Mole Templeton to make the journey in reverse, Ella thought.

They were startled once more by sounds from the street. This time it was the rumble of cart-wheels and the trotting clop of a horse's hooves.

'Now what the hangment are *they* doing at this time o' night?' Patience asked. As she spoke, and before the sounds of horse and cart had died altogether, the siren wound itself up again. On its note, this time it held steady in the all-clear. Patience said, 'Well, I don't know about you, but I'm off to bed.' At the door to the stairs she turned, hand on latch. '*Does* she feel she's not welcome?'

'Who?'

'Who've we been talking about?'

'Oh.' Ella looked across the room at her mother. 'How long is it since you were in her house?'

Patience stood while Ella willed her not to say 'And how long is it since she was in mine?' She gave the nod of one conceding a point and said, 'All right, I'll have a walk over in a day or two.'

'Shut one eye when you look at our paperhanging,' Ella said.

Four

1

Patience kept within reach the letter from Sheffield with its disturbing news of her sister. She would pick it up, turn the envelope over and put it down again. Or she would take out the two sheets of lined paper and look at them as if they held some meaning she had not yet fathomed.

Watching her, Sugden said, 'If tha *could* read, Patience lass, tha'd ha' read t'writing off t'paper by now,' and Patience said to Ella, 'Read us that bit about her leg again, Ella. You needn't read it all; just the most important bit.'

Beatie's daughter May, Ella's cousin, had written the letter. It seemed that Beatie had been having trouble for some time with an ulcerated leg. When treatment at home didn't appear to be working, and things began to get worse, her doctor had got her admitted to hospital. After some weeks there she had been informed that there was no alternative to amputation.

'But she's at home now?' Patience said.

'Yes. She's still in bed. May says she's asking to see you.'

Patience had had other things to think about when the letter arrived. It was December now, and cold. There was influenza going round and both Sugden and Ella had been down with it. Ella had spent a couple of days in bed, with no inclination to get up, while her mother fed her broth and hot drinks and kept her chest greased with vapour-rub. When the temperature fell in a sudden cold snap and the air became a raw mist, Patience even made a small fire in the bedroom grate. It cheered Ella

56

to see that glow across the room as she lay among the sweat-soaked sheets in the frowsty warmth of her bed. With her candle snuffed she drifted in and out of sleep, her thoughts, free of any immediate problem, afloat on the war, family matters, her own circumstances, the future.

She had recently done something she had told herself she would never do: she had written to Howard Strickland. Not on her own account, though, but because she had taken pity on Olive, who was frantic for news of Tony. When Ella had got a second letter to say that Howard was writing during embarkation leave she had replied, telling him that she was well, wishing him a safe journey and good luck, and asking him to remind Tony that Olive was waiting to hear (between themselves, she was desperate for word and would he send some himself rather than let Olive go on dangling).

Then there was Winnie. Of course Patience had got to know that a man had been asking for Winnie. Florrie had told her. Where Florrie had got it from Ella never knew, but the passed-on description fitted Mole Templeton well enough: 'he looked like a poacher'. Winnie smiled when Ella told her. Ella was at pains to make sure that Winnie didn't think it had come from her.

'Nobody seems to know he stopped the night, anyway,' Ella said. 'Except Arthur, and I had to tell him summat to stop him bargin' in.'

'Oh, Arthur's safe. They're all interested, o' course, because wouldn't it be nice and convenient all round if some chap did come and court me and wed me, then take me off somewhere? Just far enough for you all to forget about me.'

'I'm surprised you include me in that, Winnie.'

'No, you're all right, Ella. You're the only friend I have among 'em. But don't pretend it'd break your heart if I did move away.'

But when Ella asked if she had seen Templeton again, Winnie became curiously evasive.

'Let's talk about something else. Have you seen me new

57

frock?' Winnie ran upstairs and came back wearing a belted dress of mid-brown rayon with yellow and white flowers. She was in high spirits as she posed for Ella.

'It's lovely, Winnie. Did you buy it, or . . .?'

'Buy it nowt. I made it.' She gestured at the treadle sewing-machine against the wall. Ella had had no idea that it was ever used. 'Didn't know I could, did you? Well, I can't tailor, but I can dressmake. After a fashion.' She smiled again.

'It does suit you, Winnie.'

'Oh, aye. I'm passable in decent company when I take a bit of care.'

There were, since Templeton's visit, more and more signs that she was doing that: her hair washed regularly and brushed and sleeked back; the dab of face powder, the touch of lipstick. And she had either bought a corselette or was making a conscious effort to hold herself straight.

'A bloody fine time to start getting faddy about clothes,' Winnie said. 'If this war carries on long enough we shall all be dressing in old flour bags. It is good for morale, though, there's no doubt about it.'

Ella couldn't bring her cousin May to mind. She had an impression of a stiff woman quite a lot older than herself, in glasses.

'Did May ever get married, Mother? I've forgotten.'

'She did. Oh, she did. She wed a chap 'at worked on the railway. He was a booking clerk on one of t'big Sheffield stations.'

'They get quite a bit of free travel, don't they?'

'I believe they do. Any road, he went travellin' one day and wa' neither seen nor heard of again.'

'He just vanished, y' mean?'

'He just vanished. That's a good many years ago. They hadn't been married long.'

'No kiddies?'

'No. May hung on for a while, then she gave up her home and went back to live with Beatie and your

58

Uncle Joe. She's a typist or somesuch at one of the big steelworks. How old will she be now?' she asked herself.

'She wa' born about same time as our Ronald,' Sugden said.

'Aye. That makes her forty-six. Beatie had another before her. A lad. He died when he were only little. There were no more. Funny to think I had nine and she had only two. Shows it doesn't allus run in families.'

'Happen it's Uncle Joe's family it doesn't run in,' Ella suggested.

'Oh, Beatie allus had a bit of a maungy streak,' Patience said. 'If she made her mind up there'd be no more, she'd put her foot down and that'd be it.'

'Too easily said, Joe,' Sugden added. 'Owt for peace and quiet.'

'Well . . .' Patience fingered the letter. 'I'm trying to read between t'lines.'

'She says Beatie wants to see thee, lass,' Sugden said.

'I know, Sugden, I know. But what I'm askin' meself is this: is May saying she might get worse? Did I ought to wait a week or two an' let her come round, or should I go now, in case?'

'It's a fine time to be thinkin' o' visiting a place like Sheffield,' Sugden said.

'Why?'

'With all these air raids.'

'We wouldn't be stoppin' overnight. We'd be there and back by suppertime.'

'Who's "we"?' Sugden asked.

'Me and whoever goes with me.'

'Don't count on me,' Sugden said. 'I'm not up to it.'

'I haven't seen Beatie in – what? – five year,' Patience said.

'Your Eliza's funeral in Rawmarsh,' Sugden said.

'That's right. Will you go with me, Ella?'

'When?'

'If we get a letter into t'post tonight it should be there by Wednesday.'

59

'I don't know 'at it needs a letter,' Sugden said. 'She won't be going anywhere.'

'All t'same I'd like 'em to have a bit of notice.'

Ella, feeling quite recovered now, was nevertheless playing the rest of the week.

'When do you want to go, then, Mam? Friday?'

Sugden frowned. There was a calendar pinned to the chimney breast. He looked up at it. 'Friday's the thirteenth,' he said. 'If you want to go in t'week best make it Thursday.'

2

One way and another, with a missed connection, a porter who gave them wrong information – or information they misunderstood because he was short with them – it was nearly noon by the time they reached Sheffield. Not wanting to turn up at Beatie's at a meal time, they walked up from the station into the city centre to look for something to eat, Ella carefully holding her mother's arm in streets loud with the whine of accelerating tramcars. Cities always plunged Ella into a wondering silence as her gaze tried to take in everything that presented itself: the constant movement and changing patterns of people and vehicles, the displays in the windows of shop after shop. Of the cities she knew, Leeds lay on a gentle slope on one side of a valley and Bradford was in a deep basin; but Sheffield sprawled over several hills. At the end of streets in the centre Ella would suddenly find herself with a vista across two or three miles to where acres of terrace houses clung to a hillside, and the eye was suddenly focused by the flash of sunlight on the windows of a moving vehicle and the occasional tram would proceed beetle-like along a ribbon of road. To the east the sunlight filtered through the haze hanging over the steelworks and manufacturing plant along the banks of the River Don.

'We picked a good day for it, any road,' Patience remarked once.

Where Ella and her mother walked were posters advertising the cinemas and theatres: Errol Flynn in *Virginia City*, Shirley Temple in *The Blue Bird*; Mae West and W. C. Fields; Laurel and Hardy. There was Henry Hall in person at the Empire, with his orchestra. Jack Buchanan was coming in *Cinderella*, for Christmas, and the Lyceum was announcing *Mother Goose*. Sugden had put a folded ten-shilling note into Ella's hand before they left home and now she looked about, trying to spot a suitable café.

'What do you fancy?' she asked Patience.

'Nay, we shall have to make do with what we can get.'

'Folk wi' money can find owt they've a mind,' Ella said. 'Some of the better sort dine out every day and save their rations.'

'There's ways round everything if you've got brass,' Patience said. 'What's t'point in havin' it if it won't buy preferential treatment?'

'There's a war on,' Ella said. 'T'better sort can't fight it all on their own, so they ought to forgo their preferential treatment till it's over. Set an example.'

'An' pigs might fly,' Patience said.

She finally admitted that, given the choice, she could enjoy a piece of steak and kidney pie more than anything, and Ella kept her eyes open for a place where it might be had. A little while later they had settled thankfully enough for pork pie and peas with mint sauce in a tiny café along a passage where a cheerful woman served the customers at her four tables from behind a counter with a steaming tea urn at one end. Ella asked her what tram they should take to the district where the Widdops lived, and where they should catch it.

'From up Calderford, are you?' the woman asked.

'Near enough.'

'North o' Barnsley, anyway.' She smiled, her hands uniting cups with saucers. 'Little hobby o' mine, guessing where people come from. Different even one side of Sheffield from another, y'know. Tell Glossop Road from Brightside. I can tell when they're puttin' it on as well. Some folk come in here as though they were ordering tea at the Grand. They wouldn't be here if they could do that, would they?'

'Do they serve pie and peas at the Grand?' Ella asked, and the woman said she didn't think they did. 'There you are, then. Happen you should put your prices up. Only to *them*,' she added hastily, 'not to the rest of us.' They both laughed and felt better for it.

At the end of a twenty-minute tram-ride Ella and her mother found themselves walking along the longest street of houses that Ella had ever seen. There were three general shops along it and a pub at each end. The front doors of the houses opened directly on to the pavement. Behind them, across the main road they had just left, a steelworks clanked and clattered and thumped. Somewhere behind its high grime-encrusted wall, with broken glass along its top, a locomotive puffed and whistled. There was a different smell here: flat, exhausted. As well as pollution from the works, smoke from hundreds of domestic fires rose into what would have been crystal clear air.

'By gum,' Ella said, 'it makes you wonder if some of these people have ever seen a blade o' grass close to.'

There was hardly anyone about. Those who had been home at dinnertime had gone back to work. Ella imagined a woman in each of the houses, having half an hour with her feet up after washing her pots.

Over a shallow rise they came upon houses of a different kind; half a dozen stone-fronted semis with attic floors along an unmade cul-de-sac. They looked over a park, of sorts.

'There's your grass,' Patience said. It was an irregular oval, worn rather than mown, with a bare patch where games had been played, and a dozen mournful elms.

'They don't know they're born,' Ella said.

The houses had all seen better days, though they were roomy and well-built.

'Is it one of these?'

'Yes. Your Uncle Joe had a good job, and he was never out of work.'

62

They walked along to the first house of the second pair. Patience would have gone round the back but Ella spoke to her: 'Nay, Mother, announce yourself at the front.' Patience shrugged. 'Go on, then.' She waved Ella forward. There was a queer screw-type bell that Ella decided she didn't know how to work. So she knocked, then knocked again before they heard sounds of a chain being released and a bolt being drawn. 'All that bother . . .' Patience muttered as the door swung open.

Joe Widdop was a man of under average height, and pear-shaped. He had a high forehead and puffy cheeks. His pale grey eyes regarded them through his glasses. 'Come yerselves in. I usually call out to folk to go round to the back door, but I guessed it was you. You're looking well enough, Patience. And this'll be Ella, then. You were only a little lass the last time I saw you.'

Ella had only the vaguest recollection of him. She searched for some feature to which she might fasten identification, and found none. He was totally un-memorable in appearance. Nondescript. His trousers were held up by braces, under an open woollen car-digan. His shirt was minus collar and his feet were in carpet slippers.

'Come through,' he said. 'I've got Beatie in bed down-stairs, in the front room.' He was leading them along the hall when Patience stopped him.

'Wait a minute, Joe. I'd like to know how she is, before I go in.'

Ella thought that his eyes shifted evasively before he said, 'She's bearing up. Having your leg off is a bit more serious than a visit to t'chiropodist, but she's bearing up.'

'How far did they . . . ?'

'Just above her knee. She's full of you coming. She's talked about nothing else. We've had all the family annals, May and me. I'm pleased you've come. It'll do her good.' He put his head round a door on the right, then disappeared for a moment. They heard the murmur of another voice before he looked out again. 'Come through. She's not asleep now.'

The woman sitting up in the bed was an older and daintier-featured version of Ella's mother. Ella guessed she had been a prettier girl, too. Patience had told her on the journey how Beatie had been the one the lads all came to see. Not that, Patience had managed to convey, she was all that interested in the pleasures of physical intimacy. 'What she wanted was two or three at once, hangin' around an' admiring her. But she couldn't wed more than one, and Joe Widdop got the prize.'

'With her out of the way I expect it'd be easier for the rest of you.'

'Oh, aye. Except your Aunt Selina. She took a while to come round because she'd thought it was her 'at Joe Widdop had first come to court.'

'Oh, dear . . .'

'Aye. There was a bit of bad feeling between 'em for a while. Then your Uncle Joe got a job away and took himself and Beatie out of your Aunt Selina's sight. And not long after that Selina met your Uncle Ezra.'

There was a cage over Auntie Beatie's stump. She said that the District Nurse was coming every day to change the dressing and that wore her out so much she slept most of the afternoon. Which meant that she couldn't always sleep at night.

'Oh, but I am pleased to see you, Patience. I can't tell you how much. D'you know you were the first person I thought of when I came out of the anaesthetic? You were. And they said I'd been talking while I was under. Patience this and Patience that. And I couldn't make out why you and none of the others. I mean, I hope I'm not hurting your feelings, Patience, and I know there was a time when we were thick, as lasses; but we've done nowt in years bar swap Christmas cards. All the same it was you I was thinking about and you I wanted to see, and now you've come. And here's Ella, grown up and married! Do you know May's forty-six next, Patience?'

'Aye, Sugden said that was about . . .'

'And where's it all gone, Patience, that's what I want

to know? Where on earth has it all gone? You and me and our Selina and Eliza playing in t'Roly-poly field with ribbons in our hair. Me father walking back from Cressley market with a whole fresh fish in his neckerchief and me mam cooking it for Saturday supper. Sometimes as I've laid in bed it's seemed like only last week.'

'It wasn't though, Beatie.'

'I know it wasn't. If it was we shouldn't be old like we are.' The animation went suddenly and Beatie was weeping, her face drenched in unstoppable tears. Patience leaned forward and took her sister's hand.

'Nay, Beatie lass, we can't bring back the past. And we have a lot to be thankful for.'

'It's only seeing you, Patience,' Joe Widdop said. He had remained standing by the fireplace. Coals burned in the grate. After the walk from the tram-stop the room seemed hot and airless to Ella. She stood up and took off her topcoat. 'Give it to me,' her uncle said. 'I'll hang it up.'

'Have you got the kettle on, Joe?' Beatie asked.

'I soon can have.'

'I'd have thought you'd have had a cup of tea ready for Patience and Ella.'

'They don't want it when it's stewed and I didn't know just when they were arriving.'

'Did you get some dinner, Patience?' Beatie asked. 'Because I hope you'll stop and have your tea with us. May got a lovely pork pie. Isn't it a beauty, Joe?'

Joe, who had only just gone out, put his head back round the door. 'What's that?'

'I said what a lovely pork pie our May brought.'

'Oh, aye.'

'I don't know how it is up your way,' Beatie said, 'but there seems to be still a fair amount of pork about.'

Enough, anyway, Ella thought, for her and her mother to have it twice in the day. Yet there might soon come a time when they would consider themselves to have been lucky.

The two sisters had plenty to catch up on. Ella drank her tea and listened, speaking little herself, once she had satisfied Beatie's curiosity about Walter, except to confirm a point or jog her mother's memory about a detail. As darkness fell Joe Widdop switched on lights and drew the curtains. They talked about the wonderful convenience of electricity in the home. Joe had had the house wired in 1938. Patience said she thought Sugden was far too set in his ways to contemplate such a change, and Joe confessed that it had been May who talked them into it.

'You are going to stop long enough to see May, aren't you?' Beatie said, when Ella had made some remark about how long it would take them to get back home. 'She'll be ever so upset if she misses you.' Patience said it was up to Ella; she was in charge today. Ella said that Sugden would be sitting waiting and wondering once it got into evening. 'May only works at Hendersons, down on the main road,' Beatie said. 'Joe will have the table laid when she comes in and once tea's over May will ride into town with you and see you get your train. She always goes into town on Thursday night, to meet her gentleman friend.'

'Oh,' Patience said, 'I was going to ask you if she . . .'

'It's complicated, Patience. She's never heard a word about Herbert Tasker since the day he disappeared. Somebody saw him getting on a train at Victoria Station and that's the last anybody knows. He might have been dead and buried for years, but May can't take that for granted. Her friend's a widower and he wants to marry her, so May's involved in divorce proceedings.'

'You'd think she had ample grounds for desertion against a chap she's not seen hide nor hair of for eighteen years, wouldn't you?' Joe Widdop said. 'But the speed things move at in t'legal profession, it's going to take another eighteen to free herself.'

'Ever such a nice chap she's courting,' Beatie said. 'Quite the gentleman.'

'Works for Woolworths,' Joe said. 'Senior warehouse-man.'

He put coal on the fire from a brass scuttle. The heat of the room was beginning to make Ella feel faint. She found, too, that her imagination had started to focus on what was under the cage on her aunt's bed, and, trying to push out of her mind pictures of sawed bone and severed muscle, bloody flesh and stitched flaps of skin, she got up and said, 'I think I'll just step out for a breath of air.'

Joe opened the door for her. He put her coat over her shoulders and remained with her on the steps.

'Give 'em a chance for a quiet word.'

'Will it make her miserable that she can't get about?'

'Ch, aye. But it's a blessing it didn't happen a few years ago. We still went dancing every week when she was your mam's age. Anywhere there was a bit of old-time your auntie would ferret it out. Nights she really loved were the big dressy dos at Cutlers' Hall or City Hall. Life and soul, she was.'

'Me mam told me,' Ella said. 'She said she was quite a girl.'

'The Roly-poly field,' Joe said. 'Whatever made her think of that, I wonder?'

'She's perhaps been thinking about me Aunt Eliza.'

'Aye, happen so.'

Darkness covered the city. The moon had not yet come up and there was no light to be seen.

Joe said, 'Hard to believe there's half a million people just out there, isn't it?'

'Yes. You feel you ought to be able to hear 'em breathing.'

Joe chuckled. 'Your Auntie Beatie had a fanciful turn of mind when she was young. You've reminded me of her more than once today.'

'I'm not the belle of the ball, Uncle Joe.'

'You mean you're not as flighty as she was. Neither

was your mother. Sugden Palmer came to your grandfather's door one Sunday afternoon. He knocked and when your grandfather opened it he said straight out, "I've come to court your Patience".'

'He never did,' Ella said.

'He did.'

'Nobody's ever told me that before.'

'Well, he did. I was there with your auntie. We'd not been married long. We were just sitting down to our teas. Your grandfather was so flabbergasted he said, "Tha'd better come in, then, and we'll see'f we can find thee a plate." I don't recall that your mother said a word for the next twenty minutes; but from then on neither of them ever looked sideways at anybody else.'

'Well . . .' Ella was silent, enjoying the picture that Joe had conjured up for her.

'Now with me and your auntie,' Joe said. 'Well, there were two or three after her and I allus considered I was there to make the numbers up. Summat for the others to shine against, if you see my meaning. Because Beatrice Proctor could have wed just about anybody she liked and I remember thinking afterwards how lucky it was for me 'at folk didn't get about so far and wide in them days, or else who knows who might have seen her and snapped her up and whisked her away, eh?'

'But you got the prize after all, Uncle Joe.'

'Beg your pardon?'

'It's how me mam put it when she was telling me. You got the prize.'

'Aye. And I must have been the happiest man alive.'

'It just goes to show, I suppose, 'at people sometimes do get what they want.'

'Aye. I'm glad you came,' Joe said. 'I can't tell you how glad I am. It's daft the way families drift apart.'

'They do, though.'

'Aye.' A silence. 'Are you religious at all, Ella?'

'Not 'specially, no.'

'One of your mother's brothers had a wife who got religion. Before your time.'

'Uncle Nat,' Ella said. 'Lavinia. Me mam was talking about her not long ago.'

'So was your Aunt Beatie. Lavinia. Aye. Not much dancing after that, as I recall.'

'No.'

'May's chap's religious.'

'Oh, yes?'

'A bit too much so, for my taste. He's a steady chap, y'know, dependable; but a bit on t'solemn side.'

'It doesn't bother him that May's getting a divorce, then?'

'He seems willing to stretch a point.'

'How does me auntie's operation affect things?'

'May won't wed him till they can get a house near here. She's apparently told him so.'

Joe murmured a warning about standing too long in the cold and they were turning to go in when they heard the tap of a woman's heels approaching. 'That's May now.' She joined them on the step. 'You found us, then.' She ushered them in before her, closed the door and briskly arranged the curtain behind it. Then she switched on the hall light and smiled at Ella, who was hanging up her coat again.

'I wouldn't have known you.'

'Nor me you,' Ella said. 'Not on the street, anyway.'

She was smaller-boned than Ella remembered, but plump, well-covered, which was probably what had distorted her recollection. Her eyes were sharp and bright behind her glasses. Her glossy black hair was drawn back into a neat bun. She smoothed her snugly fitting wool dress down over her rounded hips.

'What were you doing on the step?'

'Just getting a breath of air. And letting the two of 'em talk.'

'I expect they could talk till the middle of next week.'

'Yes. But you'll understand if we don't hang about too long, won't you?'

'Of course.'

They went into the front room where Joe had opened

69

a folding table and was laying it in the middle of the floor. May kissed Patience and stood with her hand on her aunt's shoulder as she regarded her mother.

'Ooh, we have had a grand chin-wag, me and our Patience.'

'As long as you've not overtired yourself.'

Patience said they would have to go as soon as they had had tea.

'You don't seem to have been here ten minutes.'

'We can't have Uncle Sugden fretting, Mother, all the same. They'll have to come again, now they know the way.'

'And bring him with you next time,' Beatie said. 'No more excuses, tell him.'

After tea, Patience and Ella went upstairs to the bathroom in turn. It was, in truth, a bleak room, with bare painted walls and a single mat on the lino floor. But you did not have to cross a yard to get to it and Ella put one at the top of the list of things needed to improve her life, with electric light second.

As she came out she heard someone quietly speak her name. It was May, motioning to her from just inside a bedroom. Ella followed the light fragrance of fresh facepowder into the room.

'Did me dad say anything about me mother's condition?'

'Nothing in particular.'

'Well, if I tell you, you can decide if and when to tell Aunt Patience. It was gangrene.'

Ella's forehead suddenly burned. She held the bedpost and sat down, feeling the thick eiderdown give under her. She had always thought of gangrene as a condition peculiar to soldiers in the trenches, unstoppable once it took hold, putrefying the living flesh until it reached some organ that the body couldn't function without.

'They hope they've caught it,' May was saying. 'If they haven't they'll have to take off some more.' She sat down beside Ella and took her hand. 'I thought I ought to tell you.'

'Oh, yes,' Ella murmured.

'I couldn't have told you a thing like that the last time I saw you. But you're all grown up now. Married.'

'It doesn't help your plans, does it?'

'My plans? Oh, I'm used to waiting. I seem to have spent most of my life waiting.'

'I wish we lived a bit nearer. A tuppenny bus-ride. Summat like that.'

'So do I, love.' May squeezed Ella's hand before letting it go. 'Do you still like stewed rhubarb?'

'Stewed rhubarb? Whatever made you think about that?'

'It's one of the few things I do remember about you as a little girl.'

'Well . . . fancy . . . Yes, I do, as a matter of fact. I do.'

Their goodbyes said, they walked with May down the long street to the main road. A full moon was rising now in a clear sky. May stopped once to take Ella's arm and point upwards. 'Look, there's the Plough. What a marvellous night it is!' On the tram she sat, half-turned, on the seat in front of them as, behind their blinds, they travelled into the middle of the blacked-out city.

'Your mother tells me you'll be stepmother to a couple of grown bairns when you marry, May,' Patience said.

May smiled a little ruefully. 'I've a feeling I'll be a step-grandmother by the time it happens.'

'You must be making some progress, aren't you?'

'I suppose we are. But there are other complications now, of course. Still, it'll all come right if we're patient. John is very patient, thank the Lord.'

Ella found herself wishing fiercely that things would work out for her cousin, and regretting that she had not got to know her before. She was such a cheerful woman and so willing. To have had a sister like her, instead of insensitive, spiteful Doris, and Ada, who spent all her time apeing her betters and worrying about the look of things.

When they got off the tram Ella had no idea which

71

way they should go. The city after dark seemed feature-less. May got between them, pushed her arms through one each of theirs, and led them off, refusing to let go and give way even when confronted by an occasional threesome coming towards them. Because the city centre was not only blacked-out, it was teeming with people.

'By gum,' Patience said once, when they had been roughly jostled by a couple of men, one of whom had the grace to say 'Sorry, Missus,' 'there's some folk about.'

'There's some money about,' May said. 'More people in work, more money to spend. That's one benefit the war's brought us.'

Queues were forming at the cinemas and theatres. There would be the sudden jabber of voices and a gust of warm, beer-laden air as the screened door of a pub opened and shut. And it wasn't even the weekend, Ella thought.

'Will you meet your friend here in town?' she asked May.

'Yes, we shall be going to the pictures. To see Errol Flynn, most likely. That'll keep us out of mischief.'

Ella found herself wondering if that was no more than the figure of speech it usually was, or a tacit admission that May and her chap avoided being alone together in private. Then she chided herself. Not everybody had sex on the brain. All the same, though, it was a strain when you were courting a long time; and if you had a place to go to that was extra temptation, even if you were religious.

May waited with Patience in the station booking-hall while Ella went and checked their train. Then she kissed them both and squeezed their hands.

'Give my regards to Uncle Sugden and don't let it be so long before next time.'

'I'd like to keep in touch,' Ella said.

'You will keep us posted, May, won't you?' Patience said, and May assured her that she would, the sudden rising wail of an air-raid siren deadening her final words into no more than a movement of the lips and causing

Patience to jump so violently that Ella grabbed her by the arm.

'That damned thing'll be the death of me.'

'Nay, it's not siren that kills you, Mother.'

May was smiling as she shepherded them to the barrier. 'It usually goes about this time.'

'Don't forget, May,' Ella said in farewell. 'Keep in touch.' Odd that what she had at first regarded as a duty had turned into something which had enriched her life.

She looked back once they had passed through the barrier, but her cousin had gone out of the dim light of the booking-hall into the darkness of the city.

4

The only thing on their minds now was getting home. The ticket-collector had told them that the trains would keep running unless a raid took place. 'And if it does, you'll be safer out yonder than in the middle here.'

As they click-clacked out towards the city's edge the internal lights went off. A woman uttered a small shriek and a man sitting by the window let up the blind.

'Good heavens!'

Ella had noticed him when they got on: a well-dressed man with a neat grey moustache. His voice and accent fitted his appearance and contrasted with those of another man about the same age, in a worn overcoat and battered trilby, who asked now from the other side of the compartment, 'What's up, mate?'

But they could all see for themselves. At some distance separate flames flickered on the dark landscape like a pattern of small camp-fires.

'Incendiaries,' the shabby man said.

'That's what they are,' said the well-dressed man. 'So they must mean it this time.'

Ella felt the first clutch of anxiety at her heart as her mother said, 'Oh, Lord help us!'

The woman who had exclaimed when the light went

73

out said, 'Why don't they stop and let us take shelter?'

'You should ha' thought of that before, Missus. I say let's get where we're going.'

'We shan't get far at this rate.'

'I could walk it faster.'

'Somebody nip up front and tell the driver to step on it.'

There was a general murmur of laughter then when the train, as if in response to their expressed wish, began to gather speed. A few minutes later they had swung away and the fires were no longer in their view.

Ella found that once her eyes had accustomed themselves, the full moon gave enough light for her to make out faces.

Her mother said, 'I wonder what your father's doing.'

'Well, he can't know owt about this, so don't worry.'

'He'll be wondering where we've got to.'

'He would anyway, Mother. But he knew we'd be late.'

'We couldn't go straight there and back, could we?'

''Course we couldn't. Wasn't she pleased to see us, though?'

'Oh, yes. Did you like May?'

'I did. I really took to her. I wish she lived nearer.'

'No nonsense about her, though.'

'Oh, no. But it still makes you wonder why her husband walked out on her.'

'I just hope she'll get settled and be happy with this other chap.'

'Yes. Yes, I hope so too.'

The well-dressed man said all at once, 'Sssh! Listen!'

'What is it, mate?'

Ella strained her ears. She knew what the well-dressed man was listening to.

'Can't you hear them?'

The shabby man was raising the blind at the opposite window. 'Hear 'em?' he said after a few seconds. 'I can see 'em!'

Ella leaned past her mother. 'Look,' the man said,

but speaking softly now, his voice tinged with awe. She could make out nothing at first, then her eye caught something passing in front of the moon. A winged shape. And another, and another. Searchlight beams leaped up. A gun fired, with a sound almost like the deep bark of a colossal dog. Someone gasped in the compartment behind Ella. She felt the tug of her mother's hands on her clothes, seeking reassurance in contact as they tried to pull her away from the danger outside.

The shabby man had lowered the window now on his side. Cold air rushed into the compartment, bringing on it the thrum, thrum, thrum of aircraft engines. When a woman remonstrated with him he said, 'I want to know what's going on.'

'What's going on,' the well-dressed man's voice said from his corner, 'is that Gerry's out to give Sheffield a pasting.'

'Don't tell me you're surprised.'

'I'm not surprised. I'm only surprised they didn't do it sooner.'

Ella could sense an antagonism growing between the two men. She realized that each felt his rôle as interpreter of events to be challenged by the other.

'These ladies are feeling a chill,' the well-dressed man said.

'There's no chill back yonder, you can tell 'em.'

As he spoke something fell out of the sky with the hugely magnified sound of tearing calico. The explosion was muffled, distant. All the same, everyone had ducked and was now cowering, waiting for the next. The shabby man, who had pulled his head back quickly into the compartment, laughed as though embarrassed by his instinctive reaction.

'It's OK,' he said. 'It's the one you don't hear 'at's got your number on it.'

But the real raid had started now.

The train had slowed again, though it was still moving. Sitting back, Ella held her mother's hand. 'Don't worry, we're going away from it.' No sooner had she spoken

75

than the train stopped, with a groan of brakes and the chink of buffers connecting all the way along.

They were in a shallow cutting.

The shabby man said, 'Now we can't see a thing.'

'We can see enough for me,' said the woman who had spoken before. 'They want to get us out of here or take us to a shelter.'

'Somebody nip up for'ard and see if we've still got a driver and fireman,' the shabby man said, and the same woman, startled by the notion, said, 'They'd never desert us like that, surely.'

The shabby man laughed. The upper half of his body blocked the open window as he leaned out again. Patience had not spoken for some time. Ella asked, 'Are you all right, Mam?'

'Oh, them poor souls back there,' Patience said.

Yes, all going about their own pursuits, out for a good time . . .

'Sergeant!' the well-dressed man snapped suddenly.

They were all taken by surprise until the shabby man looked round.

'I'm not your bloody sergeant, mate. What you tryin' on?'

'Close the window,' the other man said, 'then we can at least try to keep warm.'

But the shabby man had turned away to speak to somebody down beside the track. He leaned down for the door handle before drawing back in and lifting the window and securing the strap.

'That was the guard. He says we'll be here a minute or two. I'm going to stretch my legs.' Ella looked out a few moments after he had dropped from sight and saw him as he stood with his back to the unlighted train and unconcernedly made water. That done, he adjusted his clothes and began to climb the bank.

There would be more of them called by nature, Ella thought, if they stood here much longer. She began to prepare herself for the possibility and asked Patience yet again, 'Are you all right?'

The raid had built now into an almost continuous rending of the air. Distinguishing guns from exploding bombs was as much as they could manage. Ella saw the figure of the shabby man as he climbed into silhouette against a glow that lit the sky beyond the dark rim of the cutting. Then, as one unbelievably stupendous explosion reached them in a shock-wave which seemed to lift the entire train and shake it before dropping it again, an intensified flare of light showed the shabby man in sharp outline as he flung up his hands before falling out of sight.

'Oh, he's hurt!'

Ella never knew what impelled her to leap so spontaneously to his aid. She did not either then or after think of him as a likeable man. But she was down beside the line and scrambling at the foot of the bank while her mother was still shaping words of surprise. There was no sign of him where he had stood, though when she reached the place she herself was illuminated from perhaps three miles away, where the something huge which had rocked them had fallen into a group of gasholders and a couple of hundred feet of flame speared into the night sky. Instinctively she shielded her eyes with her raised forearm, as though the savage heat, as well as the light, would reach and mark her. Farther over, smaller fires burned around the centre of the stricken city and even as she stood and watched, rooted by the appalling spectacle of the destruction wreaked upon the place where she had so recently walked and the people she had walked among, another wave of enemy aircraft could be heard coming in behind her.

She knew she was sobbing helplessly when the shabby man's voice spoke to her. He had to come all the way back up to her side to make her hear.

'Come away, lass. There's nowt any of us can do.'

She had scrambled right past him as he lay in the shadow of the bank.

'I was sure you'd been hit by something,' she managed to tell him.

'I just lost me footing, that's all. Turned over on me ankle.'

He took her arm and helped her down the bank. She was still puzzling over the initial spring of her action when she had climbed up into the carriage and her mother was asking her what on earth had possessed her.

'I don't know,' was all she could manage. As Patience persisted, she said again, 'I don't know, I tell you. Don't go on about it.' And Patience, unused to being addressed so curtly by her youngest child, relapsed into a puzzled silence.

The shabby man had got out a pipe. He pressed the dottle deeper into the bowl and added a few strings of new tobacco before lighting up.

The well-dressed man grabbed for the blind on his side as he said, 'Put that match out, you fool. Don't you know any better?'

'Why, half Sheffield's afire, you dozy bugger,' the shabby man said without raising his voice. 'What difference do you think my match is going to make?'

The train jolted and began to move again.

Five

1

Patience rocked and fixed her gaze on something deep in the heart of the fire. Ella wondered if she was seeing what her own mind's eye was full of, which was people from the streets of Sheffield recalled with astonishing clarity of detail, some as though seen now for the first time. There was a small smiling woman with legs too bowed to stop a pig in a ginnel; another in a fur coat and dangler ear-rings, a long feather in her hat; twin babies, one at each end of a galleon of a pram, the young mother with a brazen fag in the corner of her pretty mouth and a toddler at her knee. A one-armed man with his shabby spare sleeve tucked into his side pocket sold the mid-day edition of the evening paper. A black man crooning as he swept the street and sauntered with a swing of his shoulder behind his bin-cart. An old man, thin as a twig, who pinched the bridge of his nose and, leaning slightly forward, shot a neat gob of snot into the gutter. Men lowering beer barrels into the cellar of a pub, one of them, a huge chap of near twenty stone, laughing so much he could hardly manage what he was doing. Along a passage a man in a greasy cap and a white muffler came out of another pub followed by a scrawny woman in an imitation leopard-skin coat who screamed abuse at him. Had that tram conductor really been as miserable as he looked. His eyes when he was standing doing nothing had seemed to Ella like windows on to a tortured soul.

The snatches of overheard conversation:

'I told her, our Alice'll never stand for that . . .'

'. . . a very lustful man, is Cedric. Take my word . . .'

'He's never been near t'bloody North Pole. He's never been any further north than Pontefract.'

'I thought, you want to be careful sitting so close to t'fire with your legs open. You'll be singeing your rent book.'

'I fancied jade-green uncut moquette till I saw her three doors up takin' delivery of t'self-same thing . . .'

'Oh, Percy's done for. T'doctor told him, You're a fool if you ever play bowls again, he said, with a back like yours.'

'I never want to see anybody suffer like she suffered, Freda. I wish I thought some kind soul 'ud put me down. They don't let cats and dogs hang on like that, do they?'

'Our lot are overseas and t'Poles and t'Free French are here. Can you see any sense in that?'

'T'committee women are cleaning it through for you, he sez. There'll be no livestock by the time we move in. And there won't, because I've told him straight, I'm not going.'

Where were they all now?

Sugden looked from Patience to Ella. Ella said, as though they were alone, 'Let her be. She'll come round in time,' while wondering if she really believed it. Patience had suffered a massive shock. None of the pain and loss in her life had prepared her for the vast faceless malice of last night; for sitting in that train while the sky lit up, the bombs fell, the ground shook beneath her. And all the time, behind, in the middle of it, people they knew, whom they had only just left.

Where were they now?

The wireless said that Sheffield had been bombed for nine hours. It didn't say a lot more: there was a limit to what could be said without telling the Germans things they wanted to know. Sugden had known none of it until, unable to rest in their prolonged absence, he had put on cap and coat and walked down to the station where a passenger off an earlier train told him that Sheffield was being raided. He walked up and down the hill a number of times after that. Then it struck him that Patience and Ella might travel the last leg of their journey by bus. There was no telling. So he forced himself to remain in the house, stoically watching the quarter-hours tick away on the face of the pocket-watch where it hung by the chimney breast.

This he had told Ella when at last he heard their footsteps and met them at the door. He thought he was telling both of them, but Patience just shook her head and said, 'Oh, Sugden. You've no idea, lad.' Which was just about all that either of them got out of her for the next twelve hours.

Towards noon Ella went round to see Bobby Bainbridge at the police house. He was out. She began to explain to his wife, but got such a vague look she stopped herself short. She could see the telephone on a little shelf behind Mrs Bainbridge. All she had to do was ring the Sheffield police and ask them to look into it, when they had a minute from looking into everything else. But Ella knew that it was no use asking her.

On her way back she found herself walking the last bit behind Mildred Sadler-Browne from the big house next door. She walked with a man's stride and her head rolled slightly to her step. She was not wearing trousers so much these days. Most of the time she was seen in her WVS uniform, a mid-green tweed jacket and skirt and a felt hat with a brim, worn at a jaunty angle on her short dark hair. Checking at the pavement edge, she saw Ella and waited.

'I haven't seen you lately, Ella. How are you keeping?'
'I'm all right, thanks. Well, I'm just over the 'flu, but I'm all right now.' Ella never knew how to address their neighbour, Mildred was far too familiar and Mrs Sadler-Browne too much of a mouthful. Why couldn't she have settled for plain Mrs Browne when she married, instead of tacking on her own name as well? But the ways of the better-off were often a mystery.

Mildred asked about Patience and Sugden too, and

didn't forget Walter, explaining that her WVS work took her out much more and left her with less time to chat over the garden wall. 'So I'm a little out of touch,' she said, and smiled. Her teeth were regular but a bit discoloured, which might have been due to her smoking too much. They all smoked, the Sadlers. Even frail old Mrs Sadler was said to enjoy a fag after meals.

All of a sudden Ella heard herself blurting out the information that she and her mother had been in Sheffield last night.

'Yesterday?' Mildred frowned. 'Were you caught in the air-raid?'

'We were coming away as it started. I saw enough, though. We went to some relations of me mam's. We don't know what's happened to them. If they're safe or not.'

'They're not on the telephone?'

'No.' How many people with a telephone did Ella know? 'I've just been round to see Bobby Bainbridge, but he wasn't in.'

'I see.' Mrs Sadler-Browne studied a moment, then said, 'Come into the house.'

Ella followed her across the street, over the cobbled courtyard and through a door into a long kitchen-passage with a flagged floor and cupboards lining both walls. A tall narrow window let in light at the far end. It was the first time that Ella had penetrated the house herself. Her mother had been in, and occasional helping here had got Ada's hand in for a life of domestic service, but Ella had never got over the doorstep before. Now she followed Mildred into the main hall where the front stairs went up. There was a telephone on a table there and Mildred lobbed her hat on to the newel post and waved Ella to a window-seat.

'Better sit down. This may take a while.' She got a pad and pencil and swore when she saw that the point was broken. She rummaged in a drawer and found another. 'First off I shall need the name and address of your relatives.' Ella gave her them. 'Mr and Mrs Widdop. That's Joe and Beatrice Widdop and their daughter, May.'

'May Widdop?'

Ella's mind went blank. She felt like a child who doesn't know its lesson. 'She has a married name. Just a minute. It'll come to me.'

'It's probably not vital.'

'Well, she does live with them.' But she had not been with them when they saw her last. Oh, May, walking so jauntily off into the middle of that blacked-out city that so soon would be ablaze . . . 'Tasker,' she said. 'Mrs May Tasker.'

'Of the same address,' Mildred murmured, as if to herself.

She got the number of the Sheffield police through directory enquiries. Then she said, 'I'll wait,' turning to Ella to say, 'The line's engaged. I suppose it's only to be expected. Must be all out for everybody. Wonder how efficient their WVS branch is. Times like these when you find out what people are made of. Yes,' she said into the telephone. 'Right.' She spoke clearly, explaining without hesitation what she wanted. Mildred Sadler-Browne was a formidable woman and her voice carried authority.

'I know and I appreciate it. But my people here are worried sick for news . . . Next of kin? Of course they're next of kin . . . I know you'll do your best. Now you'll need their names and my name and phone number here . . . Yes. You are writing them down, of course . . . Is it? . . . It's a time when we all show our mettle . . . I know . . . It must be . . . If you've got all that I'll stop wasting your time . . . No, I'm relying on you . . . Just do your best as soon as you can . . . Thank you.' She hung up and patted her pockets in search of a cigarette. 'All we can do now is wait.'

'What will . . .?'

'You go home and look after your parents. When I hear something I'll come and tell you.'

Patience was where Ella had left her but there were two more women in the cottage. Ella's sister Doris and her sister-in-law, Florrie. Doris had just happened to call, but Florrie had suddenly remembered that they had planned to go to Sheffield and had become alarmed. Doris was peeling potatoes at the sink.

'There was no need for you to start doing that, Doris.'

'Nobody else was doing it and you know what time they like their dinners.'

'I ought to.'

'Well, I just thought I'd get it started, seeing as you weren't here.'

'I'm here now.'

Doris had taken against Ella at the time of Thomas's funeral and since then a lot of buried resentment had been dug up to keep the quarrel going. Apart from anything else, though, Doris was a clumsy potato-peeler, removing a quarter of the potato with the skin.

'Have you given me mam owt?'

'What should I have given her?'

'Brandy's good for shock.'

'Happen when summat's just happened.'

'A spoonful can't do any harm.'

'What do you think, Dad?' Ella turned to Sugden.

'More likely to make her sick.'

'She's got nowt in her to be sick on.'

'She wants lookin' after,' Doris said.

'I am lookin' after her,' Ella said. 'How else can I look after her?'

Patience spoke then. 'Will you two stop fratchin'.'

'You can tell our Ella nowt,' Doris said.

'You can't tell her rubbish,' Ella said. 'Talk sense an' I'll listen.'

'You should never have taken her to a place like Sheffield. You ought to have had more sense.'

'What do you know about Sheffield, Doris? Before last night it meant as much to you as Timbuctoo.'

'It wa' me 'at wanted to go,' Patience said.

'Well, she should have advised you.'

'Oh, talk about summat you know, Doris.'

'We haven't heard what happened to you yet, Ella,' Florrie said and Ella frowned.

'I'll tell you about it later.' She glanced at her mother and shook her head.

'It wa' like t'end o' t'world,' Patience said.

'Do you want a drop o' brandy, Mother?' Doris asked.

'I want no brandy. Make a pot o' tea, somebody.'

'I'm just puttin' t'potatoes on for your dinner.'

'Well make a cup o' tea while we're waitin'.'

'What did you find out, Ella?' Sugden asked.

'Nothing. Bobby Bainbridge was out and all his wife could do was stand there lookin' gormless. But I met Mildred Sadler on me way back and she took me in and rang up for me. She says she'll let us know as soon as she has some news.'

'What's all this about?' Doris asked, and Ella took a deep breath to hold her rising temper. 'Is it a secret?' Doris went on, when Ella didn't answer her.

'We're anxious about Aunt Beatie and Uncle Joe, and their May. We come away before the worst of it, but they were left with the lot.'

'If there were owt worse than that, God help 'em all,' Patience said.

'Whatever time did you get back?' Florrie asked.

'Going up to midnight,' Sugden said.

'They never should ha' gone,' Doris said.

'Oh, turn t'record over, Doris,' Ella said.

'Is anybody seein' to that cup o' tea?' Patience wanted to know.

'When I can get to the sink I'll fill t'kettle,' Ella said.

'Come an' fill it,' Doris said. 'There's nobody stoppin' you.'

'Fill it, Ella,' Patience said. 'We shall all gag if we wait for our Doris.'

Doris threw down the knife and rinsed her hands. She reached for the towel as she turned from the sink, her mouth pursed. 'Our Ella can finish t'potatoes an' all. Happen they'll taste better if she's done 'em.'

Ella looked into the bowl as she filled the kettle. 'There's only three of us, Doris. We're not feedin' t'five thousand.'

'I'm going home to see to me own,' Doris said. 'At least I shall feel useful there.'

'Oh, have a cup o' tea and don't take on,' Patience said.

'I know where I'm welcome,' Doris said.

'You know you're allus welcome here, Doris,' Sugden said, 'as long as you don't try to rule t'roost.'

'Oh, we know who rules the roost here. That's plain for all to see.'

'If you're not alludin' to me,' Sugden said, 'I can't have been puttin' my foot down like I used to.'

'Everybody knows you haven't.'

'Do they, by God!'

'Ask Florrie.'

'Don't drag me into it,' Florrie said hastily.

'As if we hadn't enough to think about,' Ella said. 'It's every time you walk through t'door, Doris.'

'It's not your door, Ella, so watch your tongue,' Sugden told her.

'I'm a married woman,' Ella said, 'and I'll speak for meself.'

'Just remember whose roof you're livin' under.'

'Don't think I ever forget it,' Ella said. 'And flamin' convenient it is for some folk.'

'Get that tea made and calm down,' Patience said, but it was too late. Ella was in full flow. Surprised as she was at the speed with which her resentment had surfaced, she was incapable now of curbing its expression.

'Nay, be damned, I had me wits nearly scared out of me last night, wondering if we'd ever see home again . . .'

'I was there an' all,' Patience said.

'But I didn't hear anybody tell you to hold your tongue.

This morning I'm running round trying to see if I can get some news to put our minds at rest, and when I come in I walk into this flamin' pantomime. Well I'll tell you again, Father – I'm over twenty-one and a married woman, and if all you want under your roof is a bairn for a skivvy, you can look somewhere else.'

Sugden was getting up. Florrie put in, 'Ella, don't say summat you'll regret, lass.'

'In future I shall say what I like.'

'No tha won't,' Sugden said. 'Not in this house.'

'There's a remedy for that.'

Sugden drew himself up. The colour had left his face. No one could quite take in how quickly it had happened. There was a time when he would have slapped her, but he balked at that now. Instead, he pushed her aside and made for the door. He wound his long woollen scarf round his neck and took down his cap. 'I s'll be in t'garden. When t'dinner's ready let me know.'

Ella had faced him down. It was the first time in her life. She felt no satisfaction. 'It's bitter cold outside and he's only just got over the 'flu.'

'You should ha' thought about that afore you let your temper run away with you,' Doris said.

Patience said, 'He was only trying to be even-handed.'

'Oh, aye,' Doris said, 'we know who he'd favour if he wa' true to his feelings.'

Ella turned on her sister. 'Listen, Doris. I can't help being the youngest and the last at home; but if you think I've got summat here 'at you're missing, then get moved back in and enjoy it. I'll flit into your house where I can have me own door and me own roof and I can say and do what I like.'

'I come here to see me mam an' dad,' Doris said, 'not to listen to your slaver.'

'Then you shouldn't bring so much of your own slaver with you.'

'You two,' Patience said. 'There's no peace when you're together nowadays. I've had just about enough of it.'

'So have I,' Ella said. 'If our Doris lets me know when she's coming again I'll make sure I'm out. And if she sees me on t'street she can cross to t'other side, 'cos that's what I shall do if I see her first.'

'Be careful, Ella,' Patience warned. 'There are some things soon said but not so soon mended.'

'Oh, be damned to it,' Ella said. 'When I think of that lovely woman we left behind in Sheffield, with her willin' nature and her smile – when I think that for all we know she might have been blown to smithereens – and I have to come home and put up with a bitch like our Doris . . .'

'I'll pull your hair for you if you say owt else,' Doris said. She was up out of the chair she had only just settled into. Ella shifted her stance slightly but did not step back.

'Oh, aye, you allus were the ready one with your claws, Doris. But if you raise your hand to me today I'll mark you, so be warned.'

Florrie was up now too, ready to step between them.

'Can't you two see how much you're upsetting your mother? Do you think she's in any fit state to put up with this carry-on?'

Ella glanced at Patience. She had her head down. There were tears on her cheeks. It was like a bad dream. If she could put the clock back half an hour, go out, come in again, refuse to be goaded. Yet there had been an immense relief in letting go. It was still uppermost, over-riding everything else. She found herself taking down her coat.

'Happen you'll all be better if I'm out o' t'way for a while.'

She had opened the door, stepped out and closed it behind her before anyone spoke again.

3

She walked away up the street because it was the only alternative to walking down it. One way was as good as another since she didn't know where she was going. Yet though she was quickly aware that walking out of the house had been easier than walking back in would be, she felt glad to be away from it, and still relieved that she had spoken out.

Friday afternoon. Most people would be at their work. She had had no dinner, and only a cup of tea and some toast for breakfast. It was cold too: not a day for hanging about in parks or on street corners. She directed her steps towards the nearest fish and chip shop, then realized that she had left her purse behind and had no money in her pockets. She could not even take a bus ride to pass the time. Pass the time till when? What did she intend to do?

Clear her thoughts. Try to work out what had made her blow up. Was it something she could change?

Winnie. Winnie would not be as newsy as Ronald's wife would be, or Florrie would have been, if she turned up with an empty belly at dinnertime. Walter's sister, either. Nellie was always pleased to see her, and so were her kids. But she did not want to explain. Nor did she want Walter's father to hear that she had had a row and walked out. It was not what they expected of her, for one thing. They knew that she could stick up for herself; but she was the conscientious daughter, not given to flying off the handle. And she couldn't have told them why. Nothing in Doris's behaviour could totally account for the way her feelings had got the better of her. No, there was something underneath, that had been building up for some time.

The plume of smoke from Winnie's chimney went straight up into the still, cold air. Frost lay in corners of the fields that the sun had not reached. Ella wished she had brought her woollen hat and scarf. And her gloves. She knocked and tried the door. The low sound she could hear as she went in was one of the children – Brian – singing to himself as he knelt up to the table and crayoned on the back of a piece of wallpaper. Ella ruffled his hair and called out 'Anybody in?' before going on into the scullery where she could hear water, and Linda, the older of Winnie's two, was standing on a buffet pretending to wash something in the brimming stone sink. Ella could not imagine how the child had managed to turn on the high old tap and was not surprised that she had not turned it fully off. Water was already running on to the flagged floor and Linda's clothes were soaked.

Ella closed the tap, pulled the plug and lifted the child down, asking, 'Where on earth's your mam?' even as she heard the tread of feet overhead. 'You'll have to have that frock off. You'll catch your death. And don't start roarin' – it's only your Auntie Ella, not the wicked witch.'

She had slipped the sodden dress off her niece when Winnie appeared in the doorway. At the same time the front door opened and shut.

Ella said, 'Who's that?'

'Only our Arthur.'

'He's in a tearing hurry, isn't he?'

'He'll be late for work. He's on afters.'

'What were you doing upstairs?' Ella said, and at the same moment her mind told her, Don't ask. Leave it alone, Ella. Mind your own business.

'Oh, he's fixing a new curtain rail for me. He likes to come and do jobs. What have these two been up to, then?'

'Brian seems happy enough. But this one was just getting the scullery nicely awash.'

'I do wish they'd taken her at infants this time. But they said they couldn't manage it till next September, when she'll be well turned five. C'mon, you, let's get you into some dry things. I don't know why your games allus have to be mucky ones.'

'Oh, she's getting into practice, aren't you, Linda? You'll happen be a grand help for your mam one day. Eh?'

She followed them into the living-room where a good fire burned behind the tall wire guard. She warmed her hands while her sister-in-law stripped the child and dried her with a harding towel.

'Don't be rough, Winnie. You'll have the skin off her.'

'Oh, she's tough as old boots, this one.'

'Where's Arthur?' the little girl suddenly wanted to know.

'Your cousin Arthur had to go to his work, pet.'

Winnie's hair fell over her face as she bent to the child. She had let it grow. It looked lustrous, newly washed.

'But here's your Auntie Ella instead,' Ella said.

'What brings you round at this time of day?' Winnie asked.

Ella was aware that Winnie was not looking at her; she who had such an open, enquiring look. I caught 'em by surprise, she thought. Arthur couldn't brazen it out, and he's smickled Winnie.

She asked, 'Have you had your dinner?'

'We were going to have some fish and chips,' Winnie said, 'but Arthur got so wrapped up in what he was doing he left it too late to go for 'em.'

'I'll go, if you like,' Ella said. 'I could enjoy some meself. T'only thing is, I've come out without me purse.'

'What's up with you, Ella? Why aren't you at work, any road?'

'I'm gettin' over the 'flu.'

'Well what are you doing wandering about at dinner-time? Did you come for summat special?' Now she did look directly at Ella as she straightened up and brushed her hair off her forehead. 'You've not brought bad news, have you?'

'No, nowt like that. Look, lend us some money if you want some fish and chips fetching, or they'll be shut. I'll tell you all about it when I come back.'

Winnie found her purse and poked coins out of it. 'I don't know where it all goes. I really don't. I hardly ever leave the house, yet I end up with an empty purse.'

'I'd pay for 'em meself, Winnie, and I will pay you back when I've got my purse with me.'

Winnie handed Ella a shilling. 'Get twice, then, and a bag of chips for the bairns.'

Ella came back expecting to find the table laid. She told herself that she should have known better when Winnie got up out of her chair on the hearth and said she would cut some bread, make the tea, and they could eat from the paper, by the fire.

'So what have you been up to? I haven't seen you lately.'

'I've just told you, I've had 'flu.'

'What are you doing walking the streets on a bitter cold day like this?'

'I've had a row with our Doris.'

'Oh, yes.'

'That's nowt, though. I've had one with me dad as well.'

She told Winnie where she and Patience had been the day before; how she had gone out this morning to try and get some news; how she had gone back to find Doris and Florrie.

'A row with your Doris is nowt fresh, is it?'

'No, but it finished with me defying me father. In his own house.'

'It's your house as well.'

'But there's only one boss in it, and that's him.'

'I know he likes to think so.'

'It is so, Winnie.'

'But you're not a bairn any more.'

'That's what I told him.'

'And you're too old to be treated like one.'

'He's got a right to the last word.'

'Not about you. He passed that on to Walter, when he gave you away.'

'Oh, did he? I've swapped one boss for another, have I?'

'That's for you and Walter to settle between you.'

'I can handle Walter. It's me dad I'm bothered about.'

'You ought to have a place of your own.'

'Easier said than done.'

'You should be in your own home.'

'On serviceman's pay?'

'You've got your wage.'

'I've no furniture, though. Not a stick.'

'Do what other folk do – buy secondhand, or get it on the never-never.'

'It needs some thinking about.'

'Start small and make sure of your independence.'

'D'you think so?'

'I know so. Let me tell you summat, Ella. If you don't watch what you're doing you might find yourself cornered.'

Ella said, 'What d'you mean?' though she knew pretty much what Winnie was going to say. She had seen that danger herself; but as a remote possibility, not something to worry about yet.

'It only wants your mother's health to fail, or your dad to need invalid care, and you'll be stuck. With you on the spot, living in, why should any of the others bother? That'll be your job. They'll wish it on you and call you all the names under the sun if you don't accept it. Show your independence now and it might not be too late. And never mind your Doris thinking you're getting all the favours. If she could see any further than the end of her nose she'd keep her gob shut and be thankful.'

'I might need somewhere in a hurry if me dad decides to throw me out.'

'I don't think he'll do that.'

'He's a proud man.'

'Tell him you're sorry and get on with your own plans.'

'I meant what I said.'

'You can still mean it when you've apologized.'

'That's two-faced.'

'The world's two-faced. It promises one thing and gives you another. You've just got to learn to live with it and get a bit of pleasure where you can. As long as you're not doing anybody any harm.'

'We can't allus tell that, can we?'

'No, we can't. Because we're only bloody human. So stop expecting too much of yourself.' She balled her fish-

and-chip paper and tossed it on to the fire with a sigh. 'I was ready for them. Did you get 'em at Websters?'

'Yes.'

'I thought so. Some folk swear by Ramsays, but I don't care for their batter. It's allus soft inside.'

'T'Neptune's not bad, but he's awful skinny with his portions.'

'What do they call him that keeps it?' Winnie asked.

'I don't know.'

'Well, never mind. He was in the Trades and Labour Club one night, Thomas told me, when one of the men got on to him. "I had fish and chips from thy premises t'other night," he sez, "an' I'd all on to find t'fish." Well, Neptune starts blusterin' and another feller pipes up. "Nay," he sez, "fair's fair. I had some and I found my fish. It were under two chips." Thomas did laugh. He could hardly get it out when he was telling me. You know he wasn't a big one for jokes and suchlike – and not dry like your Wilson – but just now and then summat would really tickle him.'

Winnie's eyes had moistened. She pressed her fingertips to them and was silent for a moment.

'Oh, God, here I am telling you to go and live on your own and I can't stand it. He could be a bad 'un when he was that side out, but I wish to God he was still here.'

She was sobbing openly now. Ella said, 'Let it come, Winnie love. There's only me to see you.' She felt in herself a sudden surge of longing to see that lost brother again.

Linda, at the table, was playing at swapping chips with Brian; a game, Ella guessed, which would end with her having more than her brother. But she looked round now and got down and came to stand, not speaking, with her head pressed into her mother's side.

'I'd like to get a job,' Winnie said after a time. 'In a factory, where I can meet some fresh faces. But there's the kids. Who'd mind them? They keep talking about opening a crêche, but they get no further with it. I could be doing summat useful and earning some money, 'stead of sitting here moping.'

Ella shook her head. She could think of no one who might look after Linda and Brian. Doris, Florrie, Martha: she could see none of them offering.

Winnie found a dog-end on the mantelshelf and lit it with a twist of paper. 'I was talking about it to Arthur.' Her tears had given way to a strained little smile. 'He said if I got a part-time job, mornings only, he'd come and see to 'em his-self. On afters he's got all night to sleep and all morning to do what he likes.'

'He'd never stick it out week after week,' Ella said. 'And I can just imagine what Martha would have to say about it.'

'Oh, it was just the goodness of his heart. I told him it was a daft idea.'

She wants to talk about him, Ella thought. She asked, 'Does he come round reg'lar?'

'He comes when he likes.'

'Do you encourage him, though?'

'I make him welcome.'

'Don't you think . . . ?'

'What?'

'It's none of my business, Winnie, but I don't think he tells 'em at home that he comes to see you. I think Martha believes he's got a lass somewhere.'

'What he tells 'em is his affair.'

'He's only a lad, y'know, Winnie.'

'He's twenty years old.'

'And young with it.'

'Old enough to go and fight and be killed.'

'They can still say you're leading him astray.'

'They can say so, but as long as he wants to come I shall let him.'

'I'm not saying there's owt wrong between you, you understand. But . . .'

'You can say what you want, Ella, as long as you don't say it to anybody but me.'

'All right.'

'There's no need for you and me to fall out on top of everything else.'

'We shan't fall out. I've said what I thought I should say.'

'You know I've allus thought you were the only friend I have in Thomas's family, and I value that.'

'I wouldn't have said what I have said otherwise.'

'No, I know you mean it for the best.'

'Well, I've said it now.'

'Yes. But it's like this, y'see, Ella. I've not had that much . . . that much affection in me life that I can turn it away.'

'Do you think I'm moody, Winnie?' Ella asked some time later.

'You what?'

'Would you say I was a moody person?'

Ella thought that Winnie had been ready to drop off in the splendid heat of the fire. It was how she had always visualized her sister-in-law when she came to mind: sitting half-asleep, smoking, by the fire, while the kids got into mischief and everything went to pot round her.

'No,' Winnie said after a moment.

'You had to think about it.'

'Oh, I don't think you're moody. I was just trying to imagine why other folk might think so.'

Walter had certainly thought so at one time. But it was only when she was being pressed to do something she could feel no more than half-hearted about. When she felt in a false position.

'You're still fed-up, aren't you?' Winnie asked.

'I can't shake it off.'

'It'll pass. God knows, you've enough reason for it.'

'Have I?'

'Well, haven't you? You went through that terrible experience last night and you're worried about your relatives. Your husband's away from home. Your wings are getting too big for your parents' house. And your

Doris is a silly cow who'd try anybody's patience.' Ella laughed. 'Have I missed anything out?'

Winnie was looking at her. Her expression seemed to say 'It's up to you whether you tell me or not.'

There was nothing else to tell. Ella was tempted for a second to talk about Howard Strickland. But that would have been merely to illustrate a bygone folly. She was over that. She had, she thought, come out of it very well. And grown up in the process.

She sighed. 'So you don't want a lodger, then?'

Winnie looked startled. 'Hell fire! If I thought you were serious I might give it some serious thought.'

'How do you know I'm not?'

'Ella love, my ways 'ud drive you ravin' mad inside a week. And it's one thing letting people know you're ready for your own home, and another getting away from your father by coming to live with me. He'd never speak to either of us again.'

'No.' Ella sighed. It was becoming a habit. 'Well, I can't sit here all day.' She paused. 'And I've nowhere else to go. Nowhere I want to go, anyway,' she amended.

'So you'd better go home.'

'Aye. But if our Doris is still sitting there, with her lip . . .'

'Look, see.' Winnie got up. 'I ought to go to the shop anyway. I'll walk down with you.'

'Oh, there's no need for that.'

'Just let me get me bairns wrapped up warm. I know your mam thinks I half-starve 'em, and never put them enough clothes on.'

She began to bustle about, lifting Brian down from the table and patting Linda's bottom. 'Go and find your coat, Linda. Your thick one that you had on yesterday.'

'Well . . .' Ella said, standing herself.

'Aye, well,' Winnie said without a smile. 'I reckon us lot'll divert your Doris's attention. And if she's gone it'll mean you're not walking on your own into a pregnant silence. As they say in them books I read.'

Six

She was dragged out of a deep, deep sleep by the pounding of a fist on the door under her room. It must have been going on for some time, for she could hear her father on the landing outside the bedroom door, which she kept ajar except when Walter was at home.

Sugden came into the room as she sat up, confused. He slid open the sash window and put his head out. 'Ho'd your noise, then. Who is it?' A man's voice answered. Ella thought she made out the word 'police'. Who else? Who else would get them out of their beds at half-past two in the morning?

She put on slippers and dressing-gown and followed her father down. He was lighting the gas and looked over his shoulder at her without speaking. She had apologized and they had made their peace; but she did not know how his permanent attitude towards her had been changed.

He opened the door and Bobby Bainbridge came in. In his tall helmet he towered under the ceiling. Had the ceiling been six inches higher he would not, Ella thought, have taken the helmet off. Who were they, after all, to be shown such courtesy?

He nodded curtly at Ella and unbuttoned his pocket to get at his notebook. 'I'm sorry to get you up at this time, but you've been making enquiries about some relatives in Sheffield.' His ginger eyebrows asked for a response.

Ella said, 'Yes. But I thought Mildred Sadler was going to . . .'

'This is police business, so they informed me.'

He had some fifteen stone of weight to match his six-feet two. There were ginger hairs on the backs of his hands. His eyes were small and blue and, Ella couldn't help thinking, rather pig-like. He wielded a lot of authority in this part of the town – his beat. There were people who admired him for it and felt safer knowing it was there. A few thought he took too much on himself. There were stories of his waylaying and beating up in the dark miscreants whom he hadn't enough on to arrest, or whom he thought it a waste of time to take to court. As for his apology for disturbing them, it was right that he should bring them whatever news he had as soon as he'd got it. All the same, he had had no compunction in waking some people up the street at three one Sunday morning when he came across the next-door draper's shop window punched in. He enjoys it, Ella thought. He's enjoying this.

Bainbridge blew on his finger-ends. 'It's bitter out. Too cold for snow.' He glanced at the dead coals in the grate. 'Be a long time boiling a kettle on them.'

Sugden gestured to Ella. 'You know where t'brandy bottle is.'

Ella got the half-bottle out of the cupboard and poured a measure into a small glass as Bainbridge lifted his hand.

'There's no need for that . . . but . . . steady on . . . Thanks. Your health.' He downed it in one, exhaled loudly, and opened his notebook.

'Mr and Mrs Widdop. Mr and Mrs *Joseph* Widdop, Number Three Peerless Street . . . I'm afraid . . .' He motioned to the brandy bottle. 'P'raps you'd like to . . .'

Sugden said, 'Go on,' but Ella felt for the back of a chair.

'Three Peerless Street was totally destroyed by enemy action, along with four other houses. Mr and Mrs Widdop have been identified.' He shook his head. 'Hadn't they a shelter?'

'She was bed-ridden,' Ella said. 'They'd taken her leg off.' Little lasses in the Roly-poly field, ribbons in their hair. While sixty-odd years later this waited . . .

99

She swallowed and managed to ask, 'What about their daughter, Mrs Tasker?'

'Sheffield have no information about her at all.'

The stairs-door opened. Patience stood there.

'It sounds like all three of 'em, Mam,' Ella blurted, and was appalled at the way her control was slipping. She began to tremble and could not stop. She pulled a chair out and slumped on to it, her elbows on the table, her face in her hands. She heard a moan and couldn't recognize it for a second as herself.

She thought, I'm not a child any more. I'm the minder, the carer. What will they do if I let go like this? Then she felt her head pulled back, the rim of a glass against her chattering teeth and the brandy burning its trail down her throat.

Part Two

Seven

1

May and her fiancé, they learned later, had been among those buried in the shelter under Marples Hotel. There were a lot of people there. It had been one of the safe places, but a direct hit had brought it all down. Joe and Beatie in one part of the city, May in another. It was a fluke, somebody said, that they should all have been killed. 'Call it what you like,' Sugden said. 'They're gone.'

Christmas was upon them only ten days after the deaths in Sheffield. Thomas was gone. Walter could not get leave. In the face of food rationing and all they had to grieve for rather than celebrate, Sugden let the Boxing Day party lapse and wondered whether this first gap in the family tradition might not be the end of it.

It was not the most appropriate time for Ella to announce her intention of leaving home. So what she found when she began seriously noting the price of furniture, she shared only with Walter, to whom she wrote early in the new year of 1941: 'I haven't given you time to think this over and you might not agree with what I'm planning. But if you do you'll have to back me up. I want it to look as if it's your idea, otherwise I don't know how I'm going to tell them, especially my father.'

'Have a look round,' Walter replied, 'and see what there is to let. Something just big enough for the two of us, and not too much for you to see to while you're still working. A one-up-and-one-down might do to start with as long as it's not a slum. We can agree about how

103

much there is to spend on furniture without busting the bank, but I shall have to leave most of the picking and choosing to you.'

She had a letter from Walter open in her hand when she finally broached the subject. It was the only way she could overcome her fear of their reaction.

'Walter wants us to look for a house.'

Sugden said nothing. Patience said, 'To live in?' giving herself time to think.

'To start our own home.'

'Whatever for?'

'Isn't it what everybody does?'

'Not when you see your husband once a month if you're lucky, and you don't know how long he'll be away.'

'What about women who marry sailors?'

'You what?'

'Daisy Marriott has a cousin who married a sailor. In peacetime, I mean. He'd go off to sea for three or four months at a time. But she had her own home.'

'You're not thinking of stopping working, are you?'

'Not likely. Not with what Walter's allowed for me.'

'You can't be starting a family, then?'

'No.'

'Have you thought what it'll be like, turning out of a cold house in a morning and coming back to one at night? Lighting your fire and cooking your meal? Just getting warmed through when it's time to go to bed? Nowt but wireless and your own thoughts for company. Eh? Why condemn yourself to all that when you've got a home here?'

'She can't stop at home forever, Patience,' Sugden said, but his face gave no indication of his feelings.

'But there's surely a better time than this.'

'Not if our Ella thinks different.' He asked her, 'You haven't got a house already promised, have you?'

'No. Walter wants me to keep a look-out.'

'You ought to let it be known, then. Himsworth, t'undertaker has some houses. So has Cassidy, t'butcher.

104

Then there's Tinner Yardley. All one side of Burden Street belonged to him at one time.'

'Loopy Lockwood has some houses,' Patience said.

'Loopy Lockwood,' Sugden confirmed. 'Aye.'

'I could never ask him,' Ella said. 'He's too daft to go last.'

'It's three parts a show he puts on,' Sugden said. 'He's not daft wi' brass. You could do worse than have a word with him. And you can look an' see if there's owt worthwhile among t'furniture in his shop, while you're at it.'

Ella studied him as he spoke. He did not look at her and still his expression gave nothing away. Sadness touched her. Whatever she did in her life she had always wished to have her father's approval; and she had just realized that with the best will in the world it would not always be possible.

2

She went to see Himsworth, the undertaker, first. 'Henry Himsworth and Nephew' it said in very nice gold letters on the shopfront. The Mr Himsworth whom Ella knew by sight and whom the rather ladylike and forbidding woman in the shop addressed as Alfred must, she thought, be the Nephew. He came across the yard from his workshop, a small, slight, grey complexioned man in his sixties, a flat cap square upon his narrow skull, a jacket over pale blue overalls and a brass-mounted folding-rule in the long pocket on his trousers' leg.

'Not at moment,' he said, drawing out the words and frowning, when Ella told him what she was after. 'We have nowt at moment, have we Thyrza?' he asked the ladylike woman.

'Can I leave me name and address in case anything comes up?' Ella asked, but neither of them made any move to take it, nor showed any curiosity in who she might be.

'Call in when you're passing,' Alfred Himsworth suggested. 'Mrs Himsworth'll tell you how things stand.' He nodded, touched his cap and went out again.

'If you'd told me what you wanted,' Mrs Himsworth said.

Were people begging for houses nowadays? Ella wondered. Weren't houses still going begging, like they had been not long ago?

It was Saturday afternoon. The day was bright and fine. There was stuff for sale stacked outside Loopy Lockwood's shop, which stood back from the street in an open yard; a table and some dining-chairs, an upholstered armchair, a brass bedhead and its matching foot, a pair of eighteen-inch tall vases with country scenes painted on them. There was a mahogany bedhead too and, as Ella took a few steps nearer to look at it, Loopy himself came out of the door.

He hailed her with an expansive sweep of his arm, his voice light and breathy. 'Nice day, Missus. Is there owt I can show you?' He had a red face and a mouth full of big white dentures. You could hear him wheezing faintly when he came close. Around middle age, he carried a bit too much weight. With his curious side-to-side rocking walk he had once, seen from behind, reminded Ella of a man-size kelly doll. Some people looked at him out of their eye-corners. He was too odd to be entirely trustworthy. You never knew what he might do. Rumours of queer behaviour in his past occasionally bobbed up in conversation. In summer he was famous for his straw boater, which he wore at a rakish angle and raised with a flourish to any woman who met his eye. Just now he was wearing a pale grey trilby which he took off and resettled as he observed Ella.

She touched the bedhead, which had flower-faces carved in its two top corners. 'It is mahogany, isn't it?'

'All the way through, young woman. Back to front and side to side.'

'I expect it's dear.'

'Depends where you've been looking before you came here.'

Loopy had had a market stall before the war, selling pots and pans. He had been noted for the tricks and dodges he employed to draw customers to him. Now, as though an audience even of one young woman was not to be neglected, he took three balls from a snooker set resting in a triangular frame on top of a cupboard and began to juggle with them skilfully.

'Would it be to replace what you've already got, or are you just starting?'

'I might be, if I had a house.'

Shyness of being cold-shouldered again prompted this roundabout approach, and she turned her back on Loopy now while she ran her hand along a chair-rail, as though she had no notion at all that he himself had houses at his disposal.

'You haven't got one?'

'Beg pardon?' Ella said, as though the subject had immediately flown her mind.

'A house.'

'Oh.'

'I've seen you before,' Loopy said, 'but I can't christen you.'

'Me name's Ella Lindley. Ella Palmer as was.'

'Aye.'

'Me husband worked in t'Co-op butchers.'

'Yes.'

'Me father's Sugden Palmer. We live next door to t'Masons Arms.'

'Aye, o' course. You lost a brother in t'pit disaster.'

'Our Thomas.'

'Yes. Aye.' He looked at her as he put the three snooker balls back in their frame. 'So do you want a house or don't you?'

'If there were summat I liked at a rent I could afford.'

'Oh,' Loopy made a gesture, 'you don't get anywhere letting houses at rents folk can't afford.'

'Have you got some houses, then, Mr Lockwood?' Ella

asked, and wondered if she hadn't gone a bit too far when he cocked her a quizzical look.

'Yes, I've got some houses.'

'Any standing empty?'

'There might be.'

Ella stepped over the threshold into the shop.

'You've got some nice things.'

'It's not everybody can see it,' Loopy said. 'Some folk want rubbish at half a crown a week just so's they can say they've got new. I look at some o' t'things in furniture-shop windows and wonder how they can call *this* a junk shop. But come in. Look round. Would it be a complete home you're wanting? I mean have you got any family heirlooms to build round?'

'I've a shoe-box 'at I keep me certificates in,' Ella said, 'and a blanket or two in me bottom drawer. That doesn't belong to me either. I mean t'bottom drawer.'

Lockwood was bringing out the dryness in her. It was at once a humorous response and a defence, in case he was thinking of trying to take her in.

He waved his arm round the shop. 'You name it and if I haven't got it I'll find it.'

Ella thought you could probably furnish a small house from this front room alone. Sideboards and dressing-tables stood next to dining-tables and three-piece suites. There were looking-glasses and lamps, ornamental flower-pots, and chamber pots with flowers on them. She nodded at a bird-cage. 'I might fancy a budgie for company.'

Loopy looked out as a man drove a horse and small flat-cart into the yard. 'Walk through there. There's more there.' He went out and began to help the man to load a dresser and an upholstered sofa on to the cart.

The room behind, through an arch, went back and back. Light got in through a big dusty window with bars across it. She had not realized how big Loopy's premises were. Here furniture was stacked high, with narrow alleys between. Tables, chairs, cupboards and chests of drawers hung over her as she made her way round and came out where she had begun.

Loopy came back. 'I knew he was due. Now we can get down to business. Have you seen owt you fancy?'

Ella laughed. 'Hang on a minute! I'm only lookin'.'

'I can get you a budgie an' all, if you want one,' Loopy said. 'Cock or hen. Yellow, green or blue.'

'Guaranteed to talk?'

'Leave it with me for a month and I'll make it talk. You might not care for what it said, though.'

'No. Well, first things first.'

'You like that mahogany bed, though, don't you? Got an eye for quality. I've the frame for it an' all. It's complete.'

'It's nice,' Ella conceded.

'Be funny if it went back where it came from,' Loopy said, but he was talking in riddles now as far as Ella was concerned.

He explained. 'An old lady died in one of my houses. Her son didn't want any of her things, so he asked me to clear it out. I haven't re-let the house yet. You can have a look at it, if you like. Nothing fancy you're after, is it?'

'Nothing fancy I live in.' She felt a flutter of excitement.

'Time for all that when t'war's over and your husband's home again, eh?'

'Yes.'

'Aye. In the meantime, though, you want somewhere to live. At a rent you can afford.' He raised one forefinger and nodded solemnly. 'Well . . .' In a corner stood a rolltop desk. It looked from the papers to be Loopy's office. He took a key out of a drawer and glanced at the label tied to it. 'Eleven Temperance Street,' he said. 'Do you know where it is?'

'I expect it's behind t'Temperance Hall, isn't it?'

'But you don't have to be teetotal to live there.' He held out the key. 'Go and have a look. No charge.'

'How much is it?'

'See if you like it.'

109

It was less than a ten-minute walk to Temperance Street. She could not remember setting foot in it before, and knew it only from the half-glances you gave the parts of your locality with which you were not involved. The square grey stone Temperance Hall had frosted windows and notices giving the times of meetings. She had no idea what went on at temperance meetings, whether hymns were sung, or if there was any religious element at all involved. The street was unmade. Motor vehicles could not get through at the further end, where a foot-path led by a grassy mound. You walked directly into the houses off the pavement and because of the gentle slope those at the far end had steps to their doors. Number Eleven, which was about halfway along, had one step. Ella stood in the middle of the street and looked at it. Sheets of newspaper were pinned across the bottom half of the downstairs sash window. There was a similar window above it and a narrower one over the front door. A fanlight of ornamental glass over the door showed that the builder had had an eye for that little extra. The houses were stone-fronted too, which raised them a cut above the ordinary. An entry gave access to the backyard, between each block of four. Number Eleven was an inner terrace house, sharing walls with Nine and Thirteen. People always said that inner houses were warmer since you shared your neighbours' heat as well. A dog, shut in one of the houses opposite, was barking without let. Three children, shouting and laughing, burst out of a door farther along and ran out of sight along the footpath.

When she put the key into the lock Ella could already hear the echo in empty rooms. She stepped inside. She was in a small lobby at the foot of the stairs. A door on her right gave on to the living-room. A door in the same wall at the back of the room made a way to the cellar-head and the back door. This was the only room downstairs: square, high-ceilinged, a sink in the corner by the window and a fireplace with a high grate and a black-leaded coal-oven. A gaslight fitting hung from the middle of the ceiling.

Before going upstairs she went out at the back. A block of lavatories stood across the yard. Somebody had painted crude white numbers on the doors. She was pleased to see that there was one w.c. to each house, and no sharing. Pushing open the door marked eleven she found a whitewashed cubicle with grit collecting on the stone floor round the base of the lavatory pedestal and damp-looking browning sheets of newspaper wedged behind the pipe that fed water down from an iron cistern. There were spider webs up in the corners. She pulled the chain and water flushed down in a healthy torrent.

She had found the lavatory key on a hook inside the back door and she locked up again before returning to the house.

There were two bedrooms, the one over the staircase quite small, though big enough for a single bed and a chest of drawers. She could detect no smell of damp but the chill of a house standing empty in winter made her shiver violently as she stood in the window of the larger bedroom and tried to assess from the state of their lace curtains the pride in home of the people living opposite. Then all at once the chill was inside her, touching her heart as she thought of the risk of her being unbearably lonely here. She had never lived alone. Born, the youngest, into the rough and tumble of a big family, she had watched numbers dwindle through her childhood and adolescence as her brothers and sisters married and went to make their own homes. But none of them had faced the prospect she was facing. She did not even know whether she could sleep in a house on her own.

111

'This is daft,' she said out loud, her voice clear and ringing inside the empty walls. 'I shall have it to master, and that's all there is to it.' Wandering through the rooms again she tried to visualize them with different wallpaper, with floorcoverings and furniture; perhaps a nice picture or two; and she came to her decision. If the rent was acceptable she would take the house and tell Walter what she had done. 'Dear Walter, Our very first address will be Number Eleven, Temperance Street, though the landlord says you don't have to be teetotal to live there. I'll tell you what it's like and what I hope we can do to it to make it better before we move in. You'll never guess who it belongs to. I was coming away from Himsworth's the undertakers with my tail between my legs because *he* didn't care and *she* looked down her nose at me for daring to want to live in one of her houses, when I . . .'

4

She walked back to Loopy Lockwood's premises. There was something going on there. Music was playing, somebody was singing, and she joined the semi-circle of bystanders gathered round the front of the shop and the clear space in which Loopy, flourishing a silver-topped cane, was cavorting to the record turning on a wind-up gramophone with a big horn.

To a bouncy accompaniment, the man on the record sang

> When I hold back a tear
> And make a smile appear
> I'm only painting the clouds
> With sunshine.

while Loopy, so surprisingly light on his feet now, strutted and two-stepped, twirling the cane, his hat-brim tipped down over one eye, perfectly aware of the

people he was entertaining but acting for all the world
as though there was not another soul in sight.

> *Though things may not look bright*
> *They'll all turn out all right*
> *If I keep painting the clouds*
> *With sunshine.*

Eight

1

'. . . take the range out that's there now and fit a Yorkist. You know, a light coloured modern range, smaller, in vitreous enamel, that still does what the other one did but looks neater and doesn't need all that arm-breaking work to keep it clean.

'Or we could really go modern and fit a tiled fireplace and buy a gas oven (if you can still get hold of one). There are some water-heaters that fit over the sink and you don't have to boil every drop on the hob or a ring. And I'm going to find out how much it will cost to have the house wired for electricity. They say it's not a fortune and it's as well to get it done before any redecorating. Imagine being able to walk into a room and get a good light just by pressing a switch, and going upstairs without a candle. (Of course you'll have got used to all that kind of thing in the forces but I hope you'll spare a thought for me.) We could even have a little electric fire to take the chill off the bedroom, and a wireless without having to get accumulators charged up all the time.

'I think Loopy will find us a fireplace and stand the expense of putting it in. It improves his property after all. But we shall have to foot the bill for the electric wiring. I asked him and he said he didn't mind us doing it but we'd have to pay for it. I suppose there's a limit to what he feels he can do for us for five bob a week. Five bob! I couldn't believe it when he said it. He said six bob when I went back and said I'd have the house. I was surprised even at that and when he saw my face he took it the other way and said straight off Oh, five then. I think it's something to do with you being in the RAF and Thomas getting killed. My father says he must have taken a fancy to me, but I'm sure he doesn't mean it that way, and I'm sure Loopy isn't the kind of man to come visiting after dark, hoping for a bit of something in return for his kindness. No, I know he isn't, so don't start worrying. I can take care of myself in that respect, anyway.

'I wish you were here so's we could go and look at it together. And then – well, you know I don't like to put that kind of thing in letters, but I do miss you and the nights are cold and a hot ovenplate isn't a patch on flesh and blood . . .'

2

Word got about. Daisy Marriott, at the mill, said in their break, 'I hear you've got one of Loopy Lockwood's houses.'

'It doesn't take long to travel, does it?' But Ella liked Daisy, who was older and sometimes good with advice, so she was not snappy about it.

Olive Sims had heard too, but she had something else on her mind. Her eyes shone in a way that Ella had not seen for some time.

'He's written.'

'Tony?'

'Yeh.'

'About time too.'

'He's in North Africa.'

'Is that where they went?'

'I've been looking at maps in t'reference library.'

'There's fighting there,' Ella said.

'I know, but we're knocking hell out of the Italians, aren't we?'

'Yes, we seem to be doing summat good there, anyway.'

'Now I've got an address I can write to him.'

Ella looked at Olive, with her thin, almost transparent skin, her narrow pink-fingered hands, and the net that held her fair hair out of danger and lengthened her slim neck to an almost ridiculous degree. Irritation blended with pity as it nearly always did in her feelings towards her. 'Does he . . .?' she began . . . 'Does he say anything about Howard?'

'He says they're not in the same unit any more. He says Howard transferred to special duties.'

'Special duties?' Ella said blankly.

'Didn't you know?'

'How could I know? I haven't had a letter for a couple of months, have I?'

'I don't know.'

'Of course you flamin' know, Olive. His letters come to your house.'

'There's no need to bite me head off,' Olive said. The colour had risen to flood her throat and face. You could tell at twenty yards when something had upset or embarrassed Olive.

'Anyway,' she said with a little jerking lift of her chin, 'now you've got a house of your own you can get your letters direct.'

And see what Walter says if one drops on to the mat while he's on leave, Ella thought; but she didn't bother to say it. She had begun to wonder if Howard might have thought better of the whole business. But was he now in a situation where he couldn't write? Was what he was doing extra dangerous? If anything did happen to him how would she ever hear about it? She could think that he had simply decided to stop writing, when in fact all the time . . .

They were all working hard. The mill was producing more blankets a week than ever before. Ella walked the duckboard between her two looms. As long as you didn't think too much about your movements they fell, as though naturally, in to a rhythm. But it wasn't natural; you had to learn it until it was second nature, then use saw you through. Now, as she brooded upon the truth,

116

that she had two men to worry about, acknowledging that despite earlier choices she couldn't just dismiss Howard's welfare as none of her business, something tipped her into gawkiness and a thread snapped. She threw that loom out of drive and concentrated on the other one while signalling the overlooker to come and get her going again.

People coming in from outside were taken aback by the level of noise in a weaving shed and did not see how anybody could speak and be heard in it. But you could, and Ella knew just what Herbert Godfrey was saying as he chewed his false teeth and rectified her mistake. She could imagine only too clearly the actual sound of his thin sour voice as he castigated her and all of them for wasting time and money, for gossiping, for always being on the chatter and natter till they forgot what they were doing. He despised women, yet they brought him his livelihood.

And all at once, to her own surprise, Ella found that she could take no more of it. She had long wanted to give him a piece of her mind, and now it came out:

'Oh, stop your flamin' grumblin' and get job done. All you can do is call women, as if you don't know how lucky you are to have so many willin' lasses. You don't deserve 'em, that I do know. All you can do is bloody whine. You want to learn to give credit where it's due.'

She didn't think that anybody else could hear, but Alice Cadman in the next aisle, the best lip-reader in the mill, had taken in every word and when she caught Ella's eye she raised her eyebrows and pursed her lips as if for a kiss. Godfrey, astounded that Ella should have spoken to him like that, took a breath and sought a response of appropriate severity.

'And if that puts thoughts of sacking into your head,' Ella said before he could utter, 'you can bear in mind that you won't be dumping me into a dole queue now, I can get another job tomorrow. You keep telling us there's a war on, don't you? Well, there is, and it means

117

that we don't have to go on putting up with miserable old buggers like you.'

She was really, she thought with vague wonder, getting very sharp-tongued these days. There was no knowing who she might tell off next.

3

Ella looked at maps too. The names in the news were Sidi Barrani, Tobruk, Benghazi. Still the Italians retreated. Newsreels showed great columns of them as they trudged across the desert into captivity. Some of them didn't look too unhappy about it. People began to say they had no stomach for the fight; it was only Mussolini and his gang who wanted the war and they were trying to ride on Hitler's back. 'A bit different from Abyssinia and shooting blackies armed with nowt but bows and arrows and blunderbusses,' Loopy Lockwood said one day when Ella was in his shop. But her pleasure in British victories was tempered, as it no doubt was for many, by the realization that being on the winning side didn't stop men getting wounded or killed.

She got on with what she had to do. For the wiring of the house Walter suggested she go to a man whose name he gave her, in the electrical contracting department of the Co-op. He was a tall man with thinning sandy hair. He scratched his long jaw without looking Ella in the face and told her that there were no materials to spare for small private jobs any longer; they needed everything they could get for their own maintenance work. 'Typical!' she exploded in her letter to Walter. 'There's committee men coming with their bags out of the backrooms in every Co-op that sells stuff either rationed or in short supply, but when one of their own who's gone to do his bit asks a small favour it's they haven't the materials.' So disgruntled was she, she didn't think of an alternative until a few days later, when a conversation at work brought a name to mind.

118

Young Clarice Mellor was telling a group of mostly older women about a lad she'd taken up with. 'I've a couple of brothers so I've *seen* one before – I mean I've caught sight, anyway – but I'd never *felt* . . . Well, to be honest, I had wondered how they could work – you know what I mean. Then when I felt it in me hand, I couldn't believe it wa' t'same thing. I mean, it isn't t'same thing is it, even though it's in t'same place?'

'What did he want you to do, Clarice?' This from Olive, whose eyes were now sticking out like chapel hat-pegs.

'Whatever it was, I didn't. But next time, I don't see how I can refuse him. It's funny, but I don't see how I've any right to refuse him. I mean, getting him all worked up like that.'

Daisy Marriott said, 'By that token you should be offering it to every other chap you pass on t'street.'

'They can get worked up just by lookin', you mean? Just by seeing you?'

'Seeing you, at any rate,' Daisy said dryly. 'I'm not so sure about me any more.'

'Don't run yourself down, Daisy,' Eva Watkinson said. 'You've still got a decent pair of legs, and I happened to hear a feller only t'other day remarking how you swing your behind a treat when you walk.'

Daisy's eyes opened wide and she flushed slightly. 'Who was that, then?'

'Ah! that'd be tellin'.'

'Y'see, Daisy, you're not for t'museum yet,' Alice Cadman said.

'But when you've been kissin' and cuddlin', an' . . .' Clarice said, still absorbed in her own affairs.

'And what, Clarice?' Olive wanted to know. 'How far have you let him go?'

'Far enough, it sounds to me,' Daisy said, 'unless she wants to find herself in t'club.'

Clarice was frowning. 'All the same . . .'

'You can't start feelin' sorry for lads that way at your age, Clarice,' Alice said. 'Take it from one 'at knows. It's no fun having a bairn out of wedlock.'

'A lass I know said it was safe as long as you did it standing up,' Clarice said, and Olive cracked out laughing.

'You tell her from me . . .' Daisy began, and Eva cut in:

'I heard about some women in Africa what have their bairns standing up. They're nomads.'

'I'm a baptist meself,' somebody said, and everybody laughed.

'What's a nomad?' Clarice asked.

'People what are allus moving from place to place. The women just crouch down, drop the kid and pick it up and walk on.'

Olive was looking at Clarice in a speculative way. Ella knew she would take her on one side later and try to get out of her all the juicy details of what she and her boyfriend had actually done.

Ella went to see Dickie Dutton, who was in the electrical business with his father. She had known Dickie since childhood. He had been a beautiful child and now, in his middle twenties, was, without fear of contradiction, the handsomest man Ella had ever seen off a cinema screen. They had gone together for a time when she was about Clarice's age and she had known with him her first intimacy with a boy beyond kisses. Their courtship had come to nothing, though. There was something missing. You couldn't spend all your time drooling over a pretty face. Dickie married Agnes Yates, someone else whom Ella had known most of her life; a girl who made no effort to hide her triumph and who seemed still, to Ella, every time she saw her, to throw her a look which said, 'I got Dickie Dutton. You didn't'. Just as Dickie himself always seemed poised on the edge of a blush, as though his instant and overriding thought when he came face to face with Ella these days was of the moment when he had guided her hand to where she could feel the startling evidence of his arousal. Surely, surely, she had thought – much as Clarice was thinking now – something as powerful and menacing must *demand* satisfaction. But Dickie had been a nice lad and, it occurred to her afterwards, probably as scared as she was of venturing further, if a lot more certain of the pleasure involved.

Those dark lashes shadowing blue, blue eyes. His straight thin nose, the way his dark hair grew so neat and close to his head; the cleft in his chin . . . Half the women in the village must have fancied Dickie at some time. But he was loyal to Agnes, even when he was being candid about her shortcomings.

'We're short of stuff, Ella.'

'That's what they all say.'

'Have you been somewhere else, then?'

'Walter sent me to t'Co-op. He thought him havin' worked there might stand him in good stead. He was mistaken, though.'

'If we don't get some essential work so's we can get hold of some stuff, we might have to shut up shop.'

'I expect they'll be callin' you up.'

'Sooner or later. It's what Agnes lives in dread of.'

'She'll have to learn to put up with it, like the rest of us.'

'She's jealous, y'know.'

'I thought her eyes were naturally green.'

'It gets hold of her, though. If she walked into t'yard now and saw us standin' talkin' she'd put t'worst construction on it she could.'

'You shouldn't be so bonny.'

'God knows what she'd go through if I went away.'

'You do this job for me,' Ella said, 'and I won't send you a Valentine.'

'You won't?'

'I won't. I promise.'

Dickie grinned suddenly. With pleasure Ella noted the effect on his face.

'I'll come an' have a look at it.'

'Come in daylight and bring somebody to chaperone us.'

'I don't want you to get me wrong about Agnes.'

'I don't. You wouldn't look the side another woman

121

was on. But she'll have to realize that for herself.' Before, she added silently, you get tired of it and go and do what she's been scared for years you might do.

4

When Walter came on his next weekend pass the work on the house was nearly complete. A gleaming Yorkist in pale grey vitreous enamel had taken the place of the big old iron range. The channels cut by Dickie Dutton to carry his electric cable had been plastered over, sanded flush and covered by new wallpaper. It was becoming the thing to colour-wash walls and that was what Ella did in the bedrooms and the staircase. But Loopy Lockwood found her half a dozen rolls of wall-paper, just enough to do the living-room. She didn't ask where he had got it and it wasn't, if she was honest, exactly the design she would have picked herself. But it looked well enough and she held her breath, because there was a big match and a lot of waste, while her mother and her sister-in-law Martha expertly hung it and finished with a couple of lengths to spare.

Winnie had offered to help Ella to decorate, as Ella had helped her. But Ella had put her off and suggested that she help her clean down instead. She did, but she brought Linda and Brian with her and they, bored in rooms which contained nothing to divert them, became a fractious distraction. For the first time Ella found the children getting on her nerves and was relieved to wave them off along the street.

Her father would not go and look at the house. Ella interpreted it as his disapproval of her leaving his roof, and was mollified when she came in one day to find him with frame and canvas, making her a brodded list-ing rug for her hearth.

'There'll not be many more o' these, either,' he re-marked as the simple diamond design with a contrasting border began to take shape. 'There'll be no old clothes to cut up, 'cos folk'll still be wearing 'em.'

Walter stood with her in the empty room.

'I wish you could have seen it as it was.'

'I can see you've done some work.'

'There were five layers of wallpaper on in here, for a start. All sorts o'patterns. One had boats going down the Nile.'

'Gerraway!'

'It did. Men rowing and black women with parasols.'

He walked round with her, discussing what they could put here, what there, what they had to have now and what could wait. 'It wants furnishing properly, though,' Walter said. 'You want to live in it, not camp out.'

'We do,' she corrected.

'We do,' he said. 'But there's no getting away from it, Ella – you're going to be spending a lot of time here on your own.'

'I know. I shall just have to think about all the other women who are in the same boat.'

He caught her as she stumbled on the bottom stair. 'You'll have to take extra care with things like that an' all, when there's nobody around to pick you up.'

His manner had been solemn but as he still held her she saw mischief in his eyes. 'The first thing we have to think about is a bed.'

She smiled. 'I know. I've got me eye on a real beauty.'

It was their first wedding anniversary.

5

Walter's sister, Nellie, made them a tea and Walter's father came in and joined them. Nellie's children, who had been all over Ella whenever she appeared not long ago, were now going through a phase of keeping their distance. 'Betsy allus were a bit on the shy side,' Nellie said, 'but now she seems to have smickled Ralph. Be thankful you can get your tea in peace. They'll come round in time.'

Ralph ran about with his arms outstretched, making aeroplane noises. Eddie Lindley said, 'Nay, your Uncle Walter doesn't go up in t'air, Ralph.'

Ella could have hit him. 'He helps to keep 'em flyin', which is just as important.'

Lindley said, 'Oh, aye,' in his self-satisfied way.

She had never been able to understand how he could disparage his own son as soon as he showed any inclination to step outside the limits Eddie seemed to think pre-ordained for him. So Walter's desire to fly might have been a bit too ambitious for a lad with his background, and somebody who knew better should have checked him before he got so far and then failed. But Ella thought Walter's ambition to his credit, not some shortcoming that his father could take pleasure in playing upon.

Only Nellie's good nature saved them; for Lindley even found room to carp when they said they were going to a Garrison Theatre concert in Calderford.

'Theatre? On a Sunday?'

'You can have a concert,' Walter said, 'but they still don't allow plays in costume.'

'All t'same,' Lindley said, 'Sunday's Sunday. Or it should be.'

'When were t'last time you were in church?' Walter asked him.

'The Sabbath shouldn't be like any other day.'

'Oh, you're just talkin' for t'sake of it. You've been known to work on a Sunday when you were called out. And for why? Because people still need their gas supply, Sunday or not.'

'There's havin' to do it and doin' it by choice,' Lindley said. 'Anyway, that won't bother you in future, whether I go to work on a Sunday or not. Or whether there's gas or not. You've had electricity put in.'

'What's that got to do with it?' Walter asked.

'It's never hurt your feelings, has it?' Ella said.

She was becoming more exasperated by the minute and felt that despite the soothing effect of Nellie's nature she would explode if they didn't get away soon.

Nellie's husband, Les Farrar, who usually said little, now put forward the argument that those who refused to buy Sunday newspapers on religious grounds ought really to give up their Monday paper, because that was produced by people working on Sunday. Lindley tried to refute this at length with an argument that Ella couldn't grasp. He had been ill and had spent a couple of weeks in hospital. It was something to do with his kidneys, but Ella wondered if it could not somehow have affected the seat of logic in his brain.

She resisted a strong temptation to criticise her father-in-law when they had left Nellie's, though Walter seemed ready to provide her with cues. Let it come from Walter itself, if it must. Who knew how far she could go before he would feel impelled to defend his father? Ella had something to look forward to and she didn't want any tension between them to mar it.

6

The theatre was packed. Tobacco smoke hung under the high painted ceiling and changed colour in the spotlights like fairy mist. The stalls were a carpet of khaki, broken here and there by the colours of women's frocks, though there were not so many of those as there would normally have been, since the soldiers were away from their homes and their wives and girl friends. The musicians on stage were in khaki too. All the men who came on to do turns were in uniform. A couple of local women singers relieved the monotony of that. One of the women took herself very seriously. She was announced as Madame Broadbent and sang songs like *Cherry ripe* and *Bless this house* with much fluttering of eye-lashes, one hand held palm upwards under her bust, as though ready to catch her false teeth should the contortions of her lips and tongue flip them free. Ella tried hard not to laugh but the shaking of her shoulder next to Walter's set him going and soon people all round

125

them were covering their mouths, one young soldier who looked no more than sixteen actually stuffing his hanky into his. The other woman had a hard, clear, true voice with which she belted out popular hits and led the audience in unison singing.

There were some solo instrumentalists too: a pianist who played Chopin and a piano-accordian player who dazzled them with pieces like *The flight of the bumble bee*, though that was not as impressive once you'd heard Harry James do it on the trumpet. And there were three comedians; two who came on and stood there and talked, and another who interrupted them.

'Are there any married couples in the house?' one of them asked.

'Yes!' Walter's arm was one of the few that went up.

'Any with a wedding anniversary this weekend?'

'Yes!' Walter's arm shot up again and Ella nudged him. 'Give up drawing attention.'

'A big hand for one of our boys in blue and his pretty lady.' There was applause, some cheers and whistles.

'How many is it?'

'One.'

'Still running it in!' Ella blushed.

'Statistics prove,' the man on stage said, 'that most British couples prefer to get married on a Saturday. Most, that's to say, except the upper classes – who always like to get the meat in before the weekend. Which reminds me – don't ask me how but it does – of the Scotsman in his kilt who presented himself at an R A F recruiting office. "Don't you think," the recruiting officer asked him, "you'd be more at home in one of your great Highland infantry regiments?" "No," said Jock, "I feel that I'm more suited to the R A F." "And why?" asked the officer. "It's because of what I have under my kilt." "What is it you've got under your kilt?" the officer asked. "I've always wanted to know." "A night-fighter and two hangers," said Jock.'

The second comedian was a bit less blue. He didn't tell gags but just stood there and pretended to read out bits from the paper. Between items he would yawn and say things like 'Confucius, he say, You can lead a horse to water, but rhubarb must be forced.' And one that touched Ella's funny-bone and set her off giggling: 'Confucius, he say, A swinging chain denotes a warm seat.'

This man eventually tried to sing and was regularly interrupted by the third comic, who reminded Ella of Frank Randle. He came dashing on carrying a false arm. 'Hitler's right arm!' he shouted, to loud cheers. The next time he was brandishing a false leg. 'Hitler's left leg!' When he appeared again he looked to be carrying nothing and the singing comedian asked him impatiently as the band stopped playing and expectant laughter ran through the audience. 'What is it now, then?' The man brought his hands into view. In each he held a pink, scrubbed potato. The audience collapsed into helpless laughter. A soldier in front of Ella looked as if he couldn't breathe. On the stage the man grinned slowly and shook his head. 'They're not,' he said, 'they're King Edwards!'

But the singing was what held it all together and lifted the spirits. They had had a First World War selection earlier, to warm them up; songs like *Tipperary*, *There's a long, long trail awinding*, and *Pack up your troubles*. Now the younger of the two women, the one with the voice that carried over all, led them through a medley of more recent favourites: *The beer barrel polka*, *When you wish upon a star*, *Love walked in*, and ending with – what else but? – *We'll meet again*.

They went out into the dark street. There was a pub directly opposite and Walter took Ella's arm and led her across to it. Inside, they squeezed through a press of khaki uniforms to a small space. Walter asked her what she would like. She shook her head and said she didn't know. She never did know. He left her and sidled and twisted his way to the bar counter. The hubbub of voices rose and fell all round her. A soldier who stepped back and nearly trod on her foot turned round and looked at her, speaking to her with some kind of southern accent: 'Hullo, darling. Looking for a handsome bloke like me?' Ella smiled. 'Got one, thanks.' They all seemed to have Royal Signals badges, all in high spirits, talking away twenty to the dozen, downing beer as fast as they could before closing time. She could see only two women. Pubs were men's places, but that was slowly changing.

Walter came back carrying a pint and a port and lemonade. Somebody jogged his arm when he was nearly to her and beer slopped over his hand. He gave Ella her glass and wiped his hand on the skirt of his tunic. She had been about to offer her handkerchief, but he shook his head. 'Only make it smell.' He lifted his glass, looking straight into her eyes. 'Here's to many happy returns.' She smiled, touched her glass to his and sipped. She had asked for port and lemon the night they were married, in the cocktail bar of a hotel on Blackpool promenade. A man had played sophisticated tunes on the piano. She and Walter were slightly uneasy, out of their element, a cold walk to Mrs Cheetham's boarding house in front of them and a bed to share for the first time. 'We've come a long way since this time last year,' Walter said now. 'Not in ways anybody else might see; but I know.'

Ella nodded. 'So do I.'

He drank in deep swallows, emptying his glass in four or five gulps, taking the edge off his thirst before going for a refill. He had time for one more before they went for the last bus. I do love him, she was thinking. It's turning out all right after all. She swapped her glass across and felt for his hand as they stood facing each other and saw the instant pleasure on his face. His eyes left hers and lingered on her mouth and throat, moving then to the vee-neck of her frock which her unfastened scarf exposed to his gaze.

The moan of the air-raid siren covered the confused din of voices, which went on without ceasing. Walter raised his eyebrows as he looked at her. 'All right?' 'I expect so.' Yet as he left her to get his second pint, images came to her of the crowded centre of Sheffield on the night of its first agony, and she felt a stir of unease. Never again would she be able to take for granted that they were 'going somewhere else'.

Walter went to the Gents'. Ella thought she would wait. Despite his keeping an eye on the time, when they went out it was to see the dim lights of the last bus receding down the hill. 'Blast!' Walter said. 'I'm sure the bugger's early.'

'They don't have to keep running at all, do they, when there's an alert?'

'No. But we've had it anyway. It looks like Shanks' pony.' It was three miles home.

'I've walked this many a time,' Ella said. 'If we step out we'll be home in three-quarters of an hour.'

'Step out too smart and we might end up in a hole.'

'It's quite light when your eyes get used to it.'

It was. Clouds slid clear of the moon as she spoke. Walter tucked her arm through his.

'C'mon, then, best foot forward.'

It gave them more time to talk about the house in Temperance Street and their plans. Sometime next week the electricity company would install a meter and switch on the power. Ella, at work all day, was leaving a key with neighbours for that. They were an elderly couple, quiet and respectable. Then she would take delivery of the furniture she had chosen from Loopy Lockwood's stock. She knew that Walter was thankful she wasn't one of those young wives who demanded nothing less than brand new, and so started with a burden of hire purchase. She had told him that she would rather have good secondhand than cheap new. The kind of furniture she did admire was beyond their present means, and that was that.

'You'll have all you want in time,' Walter promised her. 'Get this war over and we can settle down and make a right home.'

'How do you think things are going, Walter?' she asked.

'Well, we beat the Germans in the air last summer. We

129

took some stick in the blitz but it's neither stopped war production nor sickened folk. Now we're pasting the Eyeties in the desert. I haven't seen Winston to talk to lately so I don't know his latest grand plan. But things could be a lot worse.'

And at that rate, Ella thought gloomily, with nothing much happening anywhere, and nothing at all in Europe, where it would finally be settled, the war could drag on for ever. She didn't voice her thought.

Clear of the city boundary they walked along a road through what, until quite recently, had been open fields. There were still meadows and ploughed land behind the ribbon development of semi-detached houses and neat bungalows. Some plots which were not yet built on would stay like that until after the war.

There seemed to be no one else about. Not a chink of light showed from any of the houses. They had walked a little more than half-way when Walter said, 'That two pints has worked through. I shall have to have a pee.'

Ella was standing alone at the pavement edge when a man in a steel helmet and a greatcoat with an Air-Raid Warden's armband stopped his bicycle alongside her. He made her jump.

'What are you doing?'

'Ooh! You could have rung your bell and let me know you were coming.'

'What are you doing hanging about here?'

'I'm waiting for me husband.'

'Where is he?'

She tossed her head. 'Behind that hedge.'

'What's he doing?'

She had said before she could stop herself, 'Ringing up for a taxi.'

'There's no need for that.'

Walter came out before she could say, 'Ask a silly question . . .' 'Now then.'

'I just wondered what your wife was doing on her own at this time of night.'

'We missed the last bus from Calderford.'

'Where have you been in Calderford?'

'Hang on a minute,' Walter said, 'you're not a copper, are you?'

'I'm an official part-time Air-Raid Warden.'

'Well I'm an official full-time Leading Aircraftsman and this is my official wife, and where we've been in Calderford is none of your business.'

'You shouldn't be on the street during an alert.'

'We haven't heard any aircraft.'

'They went over an hour ago.'

'Well then.'

'I can order you to take shelter, y'know.'

Walter waved his arm about. 'And where do you suggest we take shelter? In a hedge bottom?'

'There's a public surface shelter half a mile up Cavendish Road.'

'We passed Cavendish Road half a mile back. By the time we'd walked there we could be at home.'

'All the same . . .'

'All the same nowt,' Walter said. 'I go back first thing in t'morning. If you think I'm going to spend half me last night here in an air-raid shelter when I could be snug in me bed and the Missus with me, you've got another think coming.'

'You're not carrying your gas masks, either.'

'Who does?'

'Them with sense. Them that knows what an air raid can be like.'

Walter was looking with new interest at the man. 'Don't I know you?'

'I don't know you.'

'You know me father.'

'Who's your father?'

'Don't you umpire in t'White Rose Cricket League?'

'Yes.'

'Me father's Eddie Lindley.'

'So you're Eddie Lindley's lad. How is Eddie? I haven't seen him since last season.'

'He's still as miserable as he allus was,' Walter said.

131

'I didn't know there was owt in cricket umpiring 'at made me like that; but you an' him's two of a kind. Give me dad a tin hat and a yellow armband and he wouldn't be fit to talk to.'

He took Ella's arm and walked her away, calling back to the man with the bike, 'I'll tell him I've seen you!'

After a little way Ella began to giggle. Walter gave a short bark of laughter. 'Bloody hell! Tin-pot bloody Hitlers. I wonder me dad hasn't cottoned on to that lot yet. He's allus twice as mouldy outside t'cricket season. Imagine him walking t'streets blowing his whistle and shoutin' "Put that light out!" Right up his bloody alley. Just his cup o' tea. Why hasn't anybody suggested it to him? Why hasn't he thought of it for himself?'

'Walter,' Ella said, 'it is your father you're calling.'

'I know,' he said. 'And I'm feeling better for it already. You can't say blood's thicker than water with me.'

As they strode along he put his hand over hers where it lay on his arm. He seemed to be charging a field of energy around himself. She felt drawn into it, the force running from him to her. The blood ran close to her skin. Her face burned in the frosty air. She wanted to shout something.

As they walked up the last rise into the village the siren commandeered the silence of the night and gave them the all-clear.

132

Nine

1

She had finished her evening meal and was enjoying a cup of tea when the knock came at the door. A sharp, no-nonsense knock. Before anybody could move the sneck lifted and the door opened.

'Can I come in?' Ella, Sugden and Patience all exchanged quick glances before turning to look at Mildred Sadler-Browne. They let her speak.

'A telephone call for you, Ella. It's your husband. Better put your skates on.' As Ella got up and went to the door, Mildred Sadler-Browne said to Sugden and Patience, 'I've been meaning to come and have half an hour with you, but I can't stop now.' She nodded and gave them a half-smile before going out after Ella.

'I'd no idea he knew your number,' Ella said.

'He'd get it from the operator.'

'I can't think why he'd have to bother you like this.'

'I expect it's important or he wouldn't have,' her neighbour said, and Ella wondered if she already knew; if Walter, to excuse himself, had told her what was up. It couldn't be anything too dreadful, though, if Walter himself was on the line. He had been at home just over a week ago.

They went along that kitchen passage again, to the hall and the stairs, where Mildred picked up the receiver and said 'Hullo? Still there? Your wife's here now.' To Ella she said, 'Take your time. I'll be in there when you've finished.'

'Ella . . .' She could not read anything in his voice as she had never heard him on the telephone before.

'How did you know this number?'

133

'I've had it up me sleeve, in case. But never mind that now.'

'In case of what?' she said, and knew that she must sound as if she was more concerned about inconveniencing the Sadlers than with what he had to say.

'I want you to get some time off work.'

'When?'

'I'll tell you exactly in a minute.'

The operator's voice broke in. 'Put more coins in the box, please, caller.'

'Blast it,' Walter said. 'I thought I had enough . . .'

'Time's up, caller.'

'Walter . . .' Ella said, and heard the click of the line going dead.

She replaced the receiver and stood for a moment biting her lip before sitting on the window-seat, her hands together, pushing her skirts down between her thighs, and looking at the pattern of tiles on the floor and the rugs which partially covered them. She was fretfully unsure what to do.

A light tread on the stairs made her look up. An old woman was descending slowly, one hand on the banister, a bag of some woven material over her free arm; a frail old woman in an ankle-length frock and a long string of beads, her hair, as always, tucked away in heavy silver skeins under a fine net. Mildred's mother, old Mrs Sadler.

'Hullo. Are you being . . . ? Is somebody . . . ?'

Ella stood up, pointing. 'I was using the phone. We got cut off.' She couldn't be sure that the old lady nowadays knew who she was. She was acutely aware, too, that she was still dressed as she had come from work and wondered if people who were not used to it could smell the mill on her clothes.

Mildred appeared.

'He ran out of change.'

'Mother, you know Ella, don't you? From next door. The youngest. The only one still at home.'

'We've got a house,' Ella said. 'I'll be off as well, soon.'

134

'I knew you all,' the old lady said, 'but I don't go out much now.' She went on and through the door.

'We eat at this time,' Mildred said. 'I insist that we all sit down together in the evening, otherwise we'd keep to our own dens in this place and never discuss anything across the table.'

'I'm in the way,' Ella said. 'I don't really know what . . .'

'Did they cut you off?'

'Yes.'

'Then he'll surely ring back. You just sit there and wait. You're not in anybody's way. When it rings, answer it.'

The phone rang even as she finished speaking.

'Yes, she's still here . . . Just let me know when you're going, Ella.'

'The bitch cut us off,' Walter said. 'And if she's listening I'll say it again.'

'Walter, are you coming home again?'

'Yes. That's why I want you to get some time off.'

'Why, Walter? What's it all about?'

There was no mistaking his sigh, because he exhaled right into her ear.

'It's embarkation leave, love,' he said then. 'They're sending us overseas.'

2

Loopy Lockwood, despite people saying he was too daft to laugh at or had a screw loose, was the person on whom Ella could rely to give her a balanced opinion of the state of the war. Her father prided himself on seeing further than the latest rumour and tried to make out a pattern behind the news, but he was hampered by his slowness in reading; whereas Loopy, when Ella called to pay her rent and another instalment on the furniture, could often be found in his half-glasses, poring over the closely printed pages of the *Daily Telegraph* or the *Yorkshire Post*.

'Now then, Ella my dear, how are things with you?

Heard from your husband yet? You will be doing as soon as he gets where he's going.'

Somewhere along the way he had slipped into the use of her first name and it was obvious that he had taken a liking to her from the warmth of his address, which was both less hearty and more sincere than his usual way with others who came within range of his patter. Yet it never got near the improper.

'They've hotted things up for him, haven't they?'

'Him and a lot more, love,' Loopy said. 'It makes you wonder where they'll open out next.'

After the stagnant months in Europe the Germans were on the move again, in something resembling their onslaught on Belgium, Holland, France and Denmark. And once they set themselves it seemed that nothing and no one could stop them.

'It's my opinion,' Loopy said, 'that Hitler's sorry Mussolini's on his side, because it stops him from invading Italy an' all.'

As it was, the Germans were reversing all the losses and defeats of the Italian forces. They had gone into Greece and Yugoslavia, and an army under General Rommel was taking back all the ground lost to the British in North Africa. Ella tried to console herself by reasoning that Walter would never be in the front line; he would never have a gun in his hands and an enemy to kill. Not like Howard.

She had had no word from *him*, either; something which, she found, didn't bother her as much as it had while Walter was still within reach. It made her wonder how many of the women she knew were as uncertain of their feelings as she seemed to be.

She saw Olive in chapel one Sunday morning, which surprised her as she had not known that Olive was a member of this congregation. But she herself had not attended a service since her wedding. Patience went to services occasionally, at times like Easter, Harvest Festival and Christmas. None of the others bothered, except Ronald's girl, Mary, who had switched from

136

chapel to church. Sugden maintained that he could not stomach being instructed in theology by lay preachers, people with little, if any, more education than himself. At the same time, his feeling that the Church of England was the preserve of those higher in the social scale effectively barred him from that. It was one of several contradictions in his life which he couldn't resolve and which he had learned to put up with.

Ella had been drawn to chapel on this day because it was the only place where she could feel joined in a common purpose with so many people at one particular time. There was comfort in it.

It was Olive's hair that she recognized first. Olive had had it cut short and dead straight; then she had put the hot iron to it, drawing it out in tightly waved strands till it stood off her head like a straw cone and reminded all her workmates of Elsa Lanchester in *The Bride of Frankenstein*. She had the pop-eyes for it too. They fixed on Ella in an unblinking facsimile of sympathy in the yard after the service.

'Not a peep from Howard,' she said. 'Isn't it funny? I mean, the way he thought about you. It must be because he *can't* write. There's no other explanation for it.'

Ella had made a point of never pestering Olive for non-existent news and Olive often looked at her as if puzzled by her patient self-control. She thought Ella was hard.

'Won't it bother you if you don't hear?' Olive asked. 'I think I'd have gone mad if I hadn't finally heard from Tony.'

Oh, no, you wouldn't, Ella thought. You'd have thought a lot about the possibility, but you wouldn't have gone over. A woman had got to have had somebody as close for as long as she had had Walter to feel his absence like a piece torn out of herself. That was loving somebody. Not loving the idea of it.

'And haven't you got moved into your house yet?'

Olive knew she hadn't moved. All the women around her at the mill knew. Ella was now making excuses not to move, though everything was ready for her. She went and put a fire in. She was going to light one now. She had time before her dinner. Olive asked if she could go with her. She had not seen the house. Reluctant for a moment, Ella then agreed, feeling vaguely that the more people who saw it the less lonely it might feel. Perhaps, she thought, I ought to have a real housewarming.

As they stepped through the little lobby into the living-room, Olive exclaimed, 'Oh, I see you've gone in for . . . for *period* furniture.'

'I thought it was just second-hand,' Ella said.

'Oh, no, it's nicer than that. Well, I mean, there's second-hand and second-hand, isn't there? You've chosen ever so well, I must say. Most of the new furniture you see nowadays looks as if it's made from tea-chests.' She knocked with her knuckles on the front of the sideboard. 'Solid. Really well made. Mind you, you've got to move with the times a *bit*.'

'Not these times, thank you,' Ella said. 'I'll wait till they're over.'

Olive took the key and went out to the lavatory. When she came back Ella had been busy, on her knees on her father's thick rug, with firelighter, paper, sticks and coal. She told Olive to have a look upstairs. Once she had got the fire burning and to a stage where it could be left, she followed Olive, finding her in the bigger bedroom, leaning on the window ledge as she contemplated the mahogany double bed and the patchwork quilt that Ella had made in several years of odd moments, since starting it as a girl in school. It was chilly up here but that had not driven Olive out.

'What a comfy looking bed.'

'It is.'

'Have you . . . ?' Olive asked.

'Broken it in? Yes. On Walter's embarkation leave. He wanted to sleep here that last night.'

And I could tell you, she thought, and you'd listen goggle-eyed to every syllable, how we made love and how as daylight came he wanted me again, and I finally had to ease him off, telling him gently, my lad, my boy, that I knew he would stay that close to me till the very last minute if he could, trying to make sure that when he did go he'd have everything of me that he could take with him, because, like me, he was struck nearly dumb with the terror of not knowing when we should see each other and be together again. But live it for yourself, Olive. I'm not against a bit of all-girls-together sex-talk at the mill; but some things are sacred.

We washed then, standing in a bowl and sponging ourselves down. He watched me and I watched him, while we said nearly nothing, except things like don't forget to lock the back door, unplug the electric fire, are you sure you're not leaving anything you'll want when you've gone. 'Only you,' he said. 'Only you.'

Then we went down home and me mam cooked us as big a breakfast as Walter's ration card and his old boss at the Co-op could get together. When I caught me mam looking at me in an old-fashioned way I felt at last that I'd done with my honeymoon, that finally I'd become in her eyes more than her youngest daughter, an independent married woman.

Now all I've got to do is find the courage to come and live here on my own.

Ten

1

Winnie sat at her table writing with a stub of pencil. 'One and a half cups water, one cup sugar, one egg . . . righto.'

Ella read out, 'One teaspoon tartaric acid, half a teaspoon lemon essence, two pint packets custard powder, two ounces butter.'

'Is that all?'

'That's all. Nobody's reckoning it's as good as pre-war lemon curd, but it's all right.'

'I don't know how much further they think they can cut everything,' Winnie said. 'It's bad enough the basics now, let alone finding treats for the kids.'

'Ada sent a recipe for wartime chocolate icing an' all,' Ella said. 'I haven't tried that so I can't vouch for it. It sounds all right, though.'

'I might as well have it while we're at it,' Winnie said, and once more wrote to Ella's dictation.

'Mix together three tablespoons sugar, two tablespoons cocoa, two tablespoons milk. Stir in a thick pan over a low light till thick and bubbly, like toffee. Then pour over cake or buns while hot.'

'. . . thick and bubbly like toffee. Pour over cake or buns while hot . . . Hmm. I'll try that . . . How's your Ada keeping? I haven't seen her in ages.'

'Nobody sees much of her these days. Cyril can't bring her like he used to, since petrol rationing. She seems to keep well, though she says Cyril's been off it. Reading between the lines I think she's wondering how long they can keep their jobs. I expect Cyril's all right. He might have to stop being a chauffeur but his boss could move him to something a younger man's had to leave. But Ada's worried that the longer the war lasts the more likely it is they'll direct female labour, and she might end up in a factory or one of the women's services.'

'Nay, how old is she?'

'She'll be what – thirty-eight next.'

'There's plenty of young 'uns to go before they get to her, surely.'

'She's married as well, which'll count. But no bairns.'

Ada was a disappointed woman. She had played her bosses' tune until her relatives were sick of hearing it: how the war would not last long because Hitler had no quarrel with Britain and there were constant negotiations for peace going on behind the scenes. Sugden became exasperated, as he always did eventually. 'What do you call bombing cities like Sheffield and Bristol and Hull – not to mention London? If you call that negotiating for peace, God help us when he means war.'

'Well obviously he can't sit back and let us build up our armaments while we make up our minds.'

'It all depends on us, does it? We just accept what he's got to offer and it'll all be over. Is that it?'

'Yes. I mean, nobody's suggesting that we bend the knee to him entirely. But I'm sure he's not an unreasonable man.'

'That's usually when me dad goes out and down his garden,' Ella told Winnie. 'I think he gets scared he might clatter her silly face for her.'

'Do you think there's a lot of well-off folk who wouldn't mind dancing to Hitler's tune?'

'Nay, don't ask me, Winnie. But I don't think Mr Churchill's one of 'em.'

'No.'

'When she was here last she was even asking what Greece and Yugoslavia had to do with us.' Ella sighed. 'I know what they've got to do with me.'

'Is that where Walter is?'

'British Forces, Middle East,' Ella said. 'It's near enough.'

They were quiet for some time before Winnie suddenly stirred. She found her cigarettes and took a light from the fire.

'Well now, I've got something to tell you.'

'Oh?'

'Sit down so's you won't fall down.' Ella waited. 'I've had a proposal.' Ella stared. 'Of marriage,' Winnie added. A little smile touched her mouth, then left it. 'Oh, I know what you're going to say. That Thomas hasn't been dead twelve month.'

'I wasn't.'

'And who'd want to marry a sloppy cow like me anyway?'

'But you're not, Winnie.'

'Don't you think so? Honest?'

'I think these past few months you've really ... well ...'

'I have made an effort, haven't I?' Winnie asked eagerly. 'It does show, doesn't it?'

'It does.'

'Aye, well.'

'Is it somebody I know?'

'You've met him.'

'Has he been again, then? Did he ... ?'

'Stop the night? Yes.' Winnie reached for her purse. She showed Ella a couple of neatly folded pound notes tucked in at the back, as if for a rainy day. 'He wouldn't go without paying his bed and board, either.'

'That's luxury lodgings money, Winnie,' Ella said.

'There were no extras in the way of personal service, if that's what you're wondering.'

'I just think you ought to be careful.'

'I am. And if you mean because of what folk might say – sod what they say. Let them live their lives and I'll live mine.'

'What are you going to do?'

'What do you think I should do?'

'There's no harm in you gettin' wed again. Your bairns need a father and you need a man to get a living for you.'

'What about keepin' the bed warm?'

'That an' all.' Ella smiled. 'It's good for the complexion.' She went on in a moment, 'Whether Mole's t'right chap is summat I can't judge.'

'They're not growing on trees,' Winnie said. 'Not that want widows with two bairns. And they'll get scarcer with this war. You know how many women were left after the last one.'

'Don't rush into it headlong, Winnie, that's all.'

'He says he'll wait, as long as he knows I'm favourably disposed.'

Ella guessed immediately that that was a direct quote from Templeton. 'Favourably disposed.' She could hear him saying it.

'I mean,' Winnie said, 'a decent interval.'

'Would you go back to the farm?'

'Oh, yes. It's not the best pay in the world but there are some little bonuses, and he's got his cottage there. Tied, of course, but he seems to have got really well in since the gaffer died. In fact, I told him if he wanted a wife he ought to be settin' his cap at Mrs Atkinson. There's not all that much difference in their ages and making her comfortable 'ud be better for his pocket than coming after me.'

'What did he say to that?'

'He said he didn't just want a wife, he wanted me.' Winnie put her head down. The flood of tears across her cheeks was swift. 'That's all I need to set me off,' she said eventually. 'Knowing somebody thinks I'm special.'

'I can't fathom folk who seem to be able to live without it,' Ella said.

'Well, anyway, you don't think it's disgusting to even talk about it so soon after Thomas?'

'No.'

'Everybody else will.'

'Nobody else need know till you're ready to tell 'em.'

'I suppose not,' Winnie said, then put her finger over her lips as a knock like a known signal came at the door – pom-tiddly-hi-ti – and a man's voice said 'Hullo!' as it opened and a hand held the blanket curtain aside,

143

then swiftly dropped it back in place. Their nephew, Arthur.

'It's still light out, isn't it, Arthur?' Ella asked, genuinely wanting to know, while also covering Arthur's slight discomposure at finding her here.

'It's not properly dark yet, anyway,' he told her.

'I've stopped longer than I intended.'

'Oh, Arthur'ull walk you to the lane-end, if you're timid,' Winnie said. 'Won't you, Arthur love?'

'He's only just got here and I've done it many a time before,' Ella said.

'Well, you won't have me jumpin' over t'wall in front of you tonight, Auntie Ella.' He even managed a smile.

Ella laughed. 'No, scared me out of me skin.'

'When was all this?' Winnie asked.

'You had a visitor,' Arthur said. 'I didn't come up.'

'Last autumn,' Ella said. 'We'd been papering.'

'Oh aye. That old friend of mine.'

'Winnie told me about it afterwards,' Arthur said.

Ella said, 'Look here, Arthur Palmer, is there some kind of class distinction round here 'at I haven't worked out?' To his puzzled face she went on, 'Why am I Auntie Ella when she's plain Winnie? And a year or two older than me.'

'Habit, I suppose.'

'He's scared of you, Ella.'

'I'm not,' Arthur said. 'Me Auntie Ella an' me . . .'

'There you go again,' Ella said.

'We've allus been pally, I was goin' to say.'

'So could you stop makin' me feel as old as Methusaleh?'

'Righto, then. I'll see'f I can get used to it.'

'I stopped him off it some time since,' Winnie said, and Ella could not stop herself thinking that it would be ridiculous to be called auntie by someone to whom you were granting intimate favours. It would be, she told herself, if that were indeed the case. And she didn't know that it was. All the same, she wondered when and what Winnie was going to tell Arthur about Mole.

144

'Aren't you going to sit down, then?' Winnie asked him.

What she didn't ask him, Ella noted, was why he had come. She didn't need to. He dropped in. His family sometimes wondered where he spent those odd hours, those unaccounted-for bits and pieces of the week. They knew he had done a job or two for Winnie, but they had no idea he called so often. Martha had speculated about a girl and, not displeased, decided to respect his privacy. His brother James had been mildly scathing about the notion. 'Our Arthur's never got a lass. He wouldn't know what to do wi' one, if he had.' And something hovered at the edge of Ella's mind, something she could not pin down about Arthur's real nature, something that might be crucial to any understanding of him and Winnie together.

'Do you want me to walk on with you?' he asked and Ella said, 'Oh, I expect I s'll manage. Take your coat off and sit down.'

As he moved behind her he said, 'You've had your hair cut.'

'Ella . . .' Ella said.

'Ella. You've had your hair cut.'

'Yes. Do you like it?'

'Yes. It looks nice.'

'D'you think I ought to have mine cut, Arthur?' Winnie asked. It was a flirtatious query, laden with mock jealousy, and Arthur, unable to match its tone, said with simple candour, 'Oh no, yours is nice as it is.'

Ella pulled a face and said, 'There you are, then.'

Arthur took a seat by the fire. He was unable to fit with immediate ease into the warm, relaxed company of two experienced women rather older than himself. A bolder lad might have teased, challenging them to define his place; but that wasn't Arthur's game. Guarded and silent, he looked from one to the other of them, his gaze not quite falling directly on either face. How shy was he, Ella wondered, when he and Winnie were alone?

'How are you likin' your new house, Ella?'

'What? Oh, well, I'm getting quite used to it now.

145

When are you going to come and do some jobs for *me*?'

'You've never asked.'

'I don't think there's owt pressing.'

Arthur was just telling her to let him know if there was, when Winnie chopped off what he was saying.

'Do you think I should get married again, Arthur?'

Ella could have gasped at the brutal directness of it. It was like an unexpected blow. She felt her own face burn as she watched Arthur's colour rise.

'I don't expect you'll stop a widder-woman for the rest of your life,' he managed.

There was the next question, the natural follow-up – Who? – but as he swallowed and met no one's eyes Ella knew that he could not ask it. And Winnie volunteered nothing more. Her gaze drifted sideways, to the fire. 'No . . .' was all she added.

Someone at that point, one of those two experienced, those knowing, teasing women, should have asked, 'When are you going to start courting, then, Arthur?' But Ella thought she knew why Winnie didn't need to, and knowing that was why she didn't ask herself. Poor Arthur . . .

'Do you want me to walk on with you?' Arthur asked, and Ella, for some reason, found herself answering curtly:

'I'm all right. That's not what you came for.'

'It's no bother.'

Did he perhaps want the chance of a word with her? 'Is me Auntie Winnie really thinkin' about gettin' married again?' No, Arthur, ask her yourself, when I've gone, and she can tell you the truth or a lie as she thinks fit. I'm just feeling my way in the dark. I don't know whether I'm imagining it all. And it's no business of mine. But I do hope you'll all be careful.

2

Walking along inside her thoughts, she found that her feet had taken her nearly to her parents' door. She turned away. She had been there once today. She called every day on her way home from work. Patience usually had something ready for her to eat. If it was ready it was harder to refuse. Ella had allowed it to become a routine, but maintained her right not to linger once the meal was over. If she couldn't learn to be happy with her own company she would be lost. They had never been given to incessant chatter, but she found the absence of anyone with whom she could share a passing thought unsettling. She relied a lot on her wireless set, a new one fed from the mains, with astonishingly good reception, and a regular change of her library book. There was little to do in the house except dust and cook light meals. Her mother insisted on washing her clothes as she had always done, though she didn't object when Ella shared the ironing.

It was spring. The weather was mild. It seemed pointless lighting a coal fire every evening. She sat now when she got in from Winnie's with a shawl round her shoulders and a bar of the electric fire on. She had lived all her life up to now in a home which had aged and renewed itself round her. Now she was surrounded by things whose past belonged to someone else. She couldn't yet call it a home; it was more like having taken lodgings. Sipping cocoa, she leafed through a magazine which somebody in the family had given Patience. Patience looked at the illustrations and the adverts, then passed them on.

They were asking women what kind of towns and cities they would like after the war; what kind of houses; what kind of kitchens and so on in those houses. Ella did not have to imagine something that didn't yet exist to express what she wanted. It was a semi-detached with bay windows, three bedrooms, a bathroom and separate lavatory, a lounge and a dining-room, and a fitted kitchen with a floor-standing gas-cooker and plenty of cupboards. In one of those cupboards would be an electric vacuum cleaner which would clean curtains and stairs as well as carpets. There might as well be a garage attached to the house also, because although she

147

couldn't envisage a day when they might own a motor car, it would be useful for storage. And gardens back and front with a lawn where they could sit out on fine warm days and where she might even serve afternoon tea when people called. No, it needed no great flight of imagination. There were houses like that not far away. All it needed was for the war to sort out other things besides beating Germany. To bring about a state of affairs where everybody had work and could save for the better things always so far denied her kind. She kept getting hints from the things she read and heard on the wireless that filled her with intermittent hope. There were voices warning against any return to the rule of the old gang. Or at least, one which didn't embody a distinct change of heart.

And central to all her personal hopes and ambitions, all her dreams of a settled and more prosperous future, was the safe return of Walter. Odd how, after all the doubts and uncertainties of her courtship and the early days of marriage, she had arrived at this ungrudging acceptance of his place in her life. She smiled as she recalled an unusually flippant remark of hers during a group chin-wag at the mill; unusually flippant because she practised a dignified reticence on the subject of her married life. 'Walter,' she had said . . . 'Walter's like parkin. He improves with keepin'.'

The electric fire had not had time to warm the whole room; it scorched her legs and face while her back was still cold. She filled a hot-water bottle from the electric kettle. She didn't mind sleeping in a cold bedroom so long as she had a warm bed; but the upstairs rooms here were colder than those at home. A good night's rest was essential if she was to carry on working at her present pace. But she had started to dream. Only since moving in here and Walter going away had she begun to dream about Sheffield and the blitz. From one of the dreams the only clearly detailed part she could recall next morning was of her standing outside Auntie Beatie's house – or the gap in the row, as neat as a pulled tooth, where the house had been – with the shabby man from the train, who was saying, 'They were going to take her leg off, y'know,' as though Beatie had been granted a happy deliverance. A couple of nights ago she had been sitting in her local cinema, only it was bigger and it had been moved to Sheffield. On the huge screen were pictures of a city on fire, with buildings silhouetted against flaming skies and firemen playing water from the top of extension ladders, all of which she had seen before. But in one bottom corner of the screen was a door and people from the audience were queuing to pass through it while Eddie Lindley, in an ARP warden's tin helmet, was ushering them along and calling, 'Step this way. Hurry along now.' Beside Ella sat Howard Strickland. He kept slapping his thigh and exclaiming 'First Class!' But Ella knew that something was seriously wrong and that the people going through the screen were deluded in thinking they were finding safety. When she saw Winnie and her children she became frantic in her need to warn her; but though she got to her feet and waved her arms about, no sound at all came out of her open mouth. 'First class!' said Howard, and slapped his knee, a cloud of dust rising from his trousers. 'Oh, first class!'

3

Ella lay in bed with the hot-water bottle behind her knees and thought about Winnie. She decided that her sister-in-law ought to marry Mole Templeton, when Thomas had been dead, say, eighteen months. If he wanted her enough to come all that way to find her he would surely make her a good husband. People would understand that she couldn't do right by her youngsters on her own. Those who were close enough to matter knew that all had not been well between her and Thomas, though they understood that it needn't stop a woman from grieving – for a failed marriage as well as her man.

149

She couldn't go on as she was. Apart from her not having enough money, she was unstable, waiting for something to happen, whether it was a good offer of marriage or the bairns to get off to school so that she could take a job. In the meantime she fluctuated between depression and grief, and something like high spirits. The high spirits Ella attributed almost entirely to their nephew Arthur. Once again she rehearsed her suspicions and tried to put her finger on that extra something which constantly eluded her, but which she felt pointed to the truth of what was going on. But what was going on? How far had it gone? Winnie was flattered by Arthur's attention; she enjoyed his company, if nothing more. But what if he had come wanting more than her friendship, different from a man's, her laugh, the warmth of her fireside, her easy-going, uncensorious personality? How different was he from other young men in their desire for sexual initiation and experience, especially if it could be acquired without responsibility? Winnie had taken herself in hand, gathered her pride so that he would not be revolted and draw back at the start. You didn't catch the smell of stale sweat on her now. She washed, had grown her hair and she brushed it till it shone. Ella imagined Winnie laughing as she realized what was happening and drew Arthur to her. Then all the subsequent moves would be hers, and once she had come to terms with the violation of family propriety she would be as warm and enveloping as the bed she took Arthur into.

Ella wanted Walter. She slid her hand between her thighs and covered herself with a still palm and fingers. She would have to stop this speculating about others' sexual pleasures. It could be pretty near unbearable with Walter so far away.

Eleven

1

In years to come all of them would remember that
time of that year, as spring moved towards summer and
their world was drenched in green; as the may frothed
in silent explosions of creamy white along the hedge-
rows and the lanes which Ella and her mates took to the
mill were thick with the trembling lace of meadow-sweet
and the dancing heads of mother-die. Not merely Mary
Palmer's wedding day, but what happened on it, searing
it deep into memory to be retained and recalled all
through that long time as years to come became years
that had gone, and heartaches dulled into the silt of
regret, where the sadness of what might have been ever
lay in wait to cloud recollections come suddenly into
mind. A long life would contain much of that, the passing years adding their own burden to that of those past,
until the time left was little more than a reflection of all
that lay behind.

2

'They don't do it in Latin do they?' Ella asked Mary's
mother. Martha had called to see Sugden and Patience
and found Ella there.

'No, that's t'Catholics. This is only Church of England.'

Mary had been going to Daker Well church, because
her young man went there. No one minded her con-
version from chapel. They were generally approving of
her having chosen such a good-living lad, who didn't
spend all his spare time swilling beer. Even Ronald,

Mary's father, gave his blessing, and he liked his ale as much as anybody in the family. In fact, he was unrivalled now since Thomas's death, and Wilson had begun to take it steady. The only reservation they had was because of Mary's age. She was only just gone nineteen.

'I thought we might ha' see one o' t'lads off first, Martha,' Patience said.

'Our James has courted two or three,' Martha said, 'but there's none of 'em got him to the sticking point.'

'He's right,' Ella said. 'Let him make up his own mind when he's ready.'

'And our Arthur . . . He's become very secretive. He tells you what he wants you to know, and no more.'

'He's a nice lad, is Arthur,' Patience said. 'It'll be a lucky lass that gets him.'

'Happen so,' Martha said. She became reflective for a moment. Patience didn't seem inclined to ask her why and Ella, not wishing to conceal in conversation information which would have added to their understanding, steered Martha back to her principal preoccupation.

'Mary wants a ring on her finger before he gets called up, I expect. There's a lot of it about. I did much the same thing meself.'

'You were a year or two older, Ella, and you'd an older head on your shoulders. Our Mary's serious minded enough, but there's summat about her a bit, well, childlike.'

'Oh, folk find that appealing,' Ella said.

'Her young man certainly seems to. He can't be near her without holding her hand. Our James said it reminded him of a picture he'd seen where a crook was handcuffed to a policeman by one wrist, and he wondered what they did when one of 'em wanted to go to the lav.' She laughed.

'I saw that picture,' Ella said.

'Aye. Anyway, I don't need to tell you what some folk are thinking.'

'Oh, there's allus some 'at'll think that kind o' thing,' Patience said. Her eye glancingly caught Ella's as she lifted her chin in the attitude of one too high-minded ever to have entertained such a suspicion. 'You've just got to let time prove 'em wrong.'

Not that the family had had no experience. A half smile played about Martha's mouth as though she was indeed remembering a swiftly arranged compassionate leave for Ronald, in 1917, so that James could be born in wedlock. And my mother carrying me, Ella thought, and in no mood to censure.

Martha was approaching her middle forties. Small and wiry, she handled her lads and her husband, Ella's oldest brother, with a dry, good-humoured tolerance which had been known to turn to ferocious challenge when she was pushed too far. Her sons were head and shoulders taller. Ella had seen James lift her under her elbows so that their faces were level. But an alert respect lived behind his laughter, aware as he was of the pain her dangling feet could inflict if he said the wrong thing. Tough, hard-working, she was Patience's favourite daughter-in-law. As company, and for good sense, she preferred her to her daughters Ada and Doris.

Mary was another Co-op employee, to be found at Daker Well branch grocery. Her fiancé, Trevor Butterworth, worked for a jobbing builder whose premises were just across the way. All so neat and tidy; everything within an arm's length, including the church where they were to be married.

Mary was going to live with Trevor's people for the time being.

'You'll lose a useful pair of hands,' Patience said. 'A pair of lads takes some cleaning up after.'

'Cleaning after 'em and trying to fill 'em up,' Martha said.

'Who can fill any man's belly with what they expect us to live on now?' Patience paused, then hinted, 'And I expect Mary 'ull be taking her little extras where she's going.'

153

'Not so many little extras,' Martha said. 'She's not first in line down there. No, nor second either.' She got up. 'Anyway, you've got a date for your calendar.'

'How many's comin'?'

'Well, Ronald said he'd only one lass, so he'd put his hand down and invite you all.'

'By gum,' Patience said. 'D'you hear that, Sugden?'

'I heard.'

'All the same,' Martha said, 'I expect I shall have to top up what he gives me with me cleaning money. He knows I have it, y'see, and he'll never rest till he thinks it's all spent. Ronald doesn't agree with married women havin' independent means.'

Ella laughed and Martha grinned with her.

'Tha makes it sound like dividends from t'stock market, Martha lass,' Sugden said.

'Aye, well, I'm knocking it off when our Mary's gone. By the way, I've lost your Ada's address. Can you jot it down for me, Ella? And will you tell Winnie when you see her? It'll save me trailing there, and I'm not spending postage on folk what live near.'

Even you, Ella thought. Even you think something less will be enough for Winnie. Because I'll bet you wouldn't do that to somebody like our Doris.

Martha went.

'She'll be on the go now from morn till night till it's all over,' Patience said.

'And loving every minute of it,' Ella said.

'Martha's not built for putting her feet up.'

'That bairn's *not* expecting, is she?' Sugden wanted to know.

'O' course she isn't, Sugden.'

'Because if she is I'd better be knowing. I don't want to be sayin' t'wrong thing.'

'Well, she isn't. You heard what Martha said.'

'An' o' course, you never thought so for a minute.'

'Of course I didn't. I leave all that sort o' thing to other folk.'

Mary's cousins Catherine and Audrey were bridesmaids.
A third was the girl who had lost her father's tripe
down the drain. Ella got her on one side outside the
church, between photographs.

'By gum, but you're on 'em nearly all, aren't you?'

'Yes.'

'Isn't your name Mary as well?'

'Yes, Mary Butterworth.'

'There'll be two Mary Butterworths in Daker now,
won't there? Folk'll be gettin' you mixed up.'

'She's Mrs Butterworth and I'm Miss.'

'Yes, o' course. And I suppose you an' me's related
now.'

'Are we? What are we?'

'Well, Trevor's your cousin and Mary's my niece,
so . . .'

'You're just my cousin-in-law's auntie and I'm your
nephew-in-law's cousin.'

'By, but you're sharp.'

'We've been doin' family trees at school.'

'Have you?' Ella looked round to make sure they could
not be overheard. 'Did anybody ever find out about that
tripe?'

'No. And you won't let on to anybody today, will you?'

'Why should I suddenly let on today?'

'People at weddings get drinkin' sherry wine and they
say all sorts o' things.'

'Do they? You sound as if you know. Have you been
a bridesmaid before?'

'Twice.'

'How old are you?'

'Nearly nine.'

'H'mm. It'll be your turn before you know it. Who do
you fancy at present? Our Granville?'

'He's too clever.'

'I'll bet he couldn't have worked out how we're not related any faster than you did.'

'He'll be going to t'grammar school next year.'

'If he passes.'

'Oh, he'll pass.'

'Won't you be goin'?'

'I don't think so. Me dad says lettin' lasses stop at school till they're sixteen is a waste of time.'

'Which is your dad? Is he here?'

Mary looked round as the bride and bridegroom posed alone before the church door. 'That's him, over there, talkin' to Trevor's mother.' Ella saw a lean man a little under middle height with a scrawny neck in a white collar too big for it and a tuft of sandy hair. He stood with his shoulders back and his narrow chest thrown out.

'Well, he doesn't look so flae'some.'

'He is, though. He's got an awful temper and his hands are as hard as iron.'

'H'mm. Listen, they're wanting you again.'

Another group was being arranged, of bride and groom, best man, both sets of parents and the three bridesmaids. The photographer had got everything to his satisfaction and was about to press the button when Doris fussed into shot to fiddle with her daughter Audrey's dress and bouquet. Ella had found herself sitting next to Doris in church, but Doris had moved Neville between them and they had managed without speaking. She was wearing a pale blue straw hat and as she was about to straighten up Audrey made an impatient movement which dislodged it and tipped it to one side. Ella smiled.

She looked over the group and at the people standing about the churchyard. She liked to see the people she knew and saw often dressed up occasionally. Rationing and shortages had not yet seriously affected their glad rags: most of them had clothes bought or made before the war. Ella was wearing the costume she had gone away on honeymoon in. Her sister Ada had on the lilac outfit she had worn that day.

Martha was delighted that Ada and Cyril had come. It was one thing nipping over from Harrogate in your boss's motor car, another making the journey by train, with two changes.

James came up to Ella. 'Now then, auntie.'

'I'll give you auntie.'

'Lovely day for it.'

Ella saw with a new awareness how James resembled his father in the way he stood and moved his head. He even had Ronald's way of holding a lighted cigarette with the burning end inside his cupped palm. He seemed to be alone.

'Where's your lady friend today?'

'Which one's that?'

'Nay, how many do you reckon to be engaged to?'

'If they want to reckon they're engaged that's up to them.'

'All right for t'jeweller, or do you keep t'same ring for 'em all?'

'There's only one of 'em had a ring, an' she's still got it.'

'Well,' Ella said, 'it'd be handy if you could make your mind up while we've all got summat to wear.'

'I allus thought you were on my side.'

'It depends who I'm talking to. And I am a woman, y'know. It makes a difference.'

'Just now you sound like an auntie. A real old one.'

Ella laughed. 'I'm only interested in your welfare.'

'Know what's good for me, do you?'

' 'Course I do.'

'All it's cracked up to be, is it, marriage?'

'Better than some folk make out.'

'You'd better tell our Arthur, then.'

'Oh? Why?'

He was eyeing her quizzically now. 'Have you met his woman?'

'Has he got one?'

'I thought you might know.'

'I'm surprised if you don't.'

'You mean he has?'

157

'I mean whether he has or not.'

His eyes lingered on her face for a moment longer. Then he shrugged. 'Oh, we don't work at same pit any more. And we're on different shifts. I can't spend my time trailing after him.'

'Why should you?'

'Because he acts like he's ashamed of her. If there *is* a her.'

'Aye, if.'

Looking past him Ella suddenly became aware of Winnie. Standing alone, she was apparently absorbed in watching the photographs being taken. But even from here Ella could see that her eyes had stopped registering what was in front of them and were turned inwards on to something that, in its visible expression, all at once chilled the sun's warmth out of Ella's spine. She would have gone to her, and had shifted the weight on her feet in readiness, when James twisted his head and stepped to one side before her and showed her Arthur, also alone, also seeing what she had just seen, for a few seconds before someone's cackling laugh snapped the lines of tension and he turned his face towards Ella, as though realizing he was observed, yet no more aware that his eyes were on her than he was, for now, of anybody else around him.

4

Ada loved a church wedding. Chapel had been good enough for her as a girl, but now she loved all the extras that made the members of her family feel slightly ill-at-ease, the high altar, the stained glass, the ornately carved screens, the choirboys in their white surplices, the vicar in his, with a broad ribbon round his shoulders whose colour, Ada maintained, told you which university he'd been to. Nobody had actually started chanting, but Ella had felt they might at any moment, and the vicar conducted the service in a sing-song which invested it with a remote kind of importance, but bleached it of human warmth.

It was Ada and Cyril who stood talking to the vicar after the ceremony. As they were not needed for the photographs they had plenty of opportunity to make his acquaintance. He was a tall man of about forty, already bald at the front but with thick hair growing out of his nostrils. He smoked a pipe and was known to have an occasional drink standing up in the bar of the Conservative Club, which wasn't at all like the behaviour of the local Methodist ministers and, for Ella's family, cast grave doubts upon his sincerity.

He came to the reception and said grace before the meal. There was sherry and port for the women and bottled beer for the men, which was a division according to general taste, though the vicar had a couple of glasses of sherry before sitting down and Ella noted that Winnie had taken a glass of beer.

Winnie was thought of as a person who cried at weddings and might embarrass them all in some way at any time. She had wept bitter tears at Ella's wedding, while Thomas was still alive. So when Florrie came back from the ladies and said that Winnie was in there weeping, nobody was especially surprised or concerned.

'Is she all right?' Ella asked.

'Oh aye,' Florrie said. 'It's not long, is it, after all, since she lost him?'

Arthur was amusing Winnie's children by some simple sleight of hand, making coins vanish and reappear . . .

'He's got a way with 'em, hasn't he?' Florrie said, nodding her head at him. 'I didn't know he did party tricks.'

'We've stopped having parties,' Ella said. 'That might be why.'

'Aye . . .' Florrie looked suddenly regretful. 'They were good times, weren't they, your mam an' dad's Boxing Day dos? Now all we do is get together at weddings and . . .' She stopped. 'But we don't want to talk about the other sort, do we? Not with all 'at's going on in the

159

world. I know it might sound selfish, but I thank the Lord in every prayer 'at our George and Granville are too young for it and with a bit o'luck it'll be over before they're old enough.'

Ella said, 'Oh, surely.' George, the older of Florrie's two lads wasn't yet fifteen. 'And don't you worry, Florrie, I don't blame you for being thankful.'

She was thinking that she might go to Winnie. She wanted the lavatory anyway. But she was distracted as she moved along the table by a huddle at the end which included the vicar, Sudgen, Trevor Butterworth's father and Ada. Ada had been full of I-told-you-so since first arriving, though only now had she got a group to go at. Rudolf Hess, one of the top Nazis, had flown over single-handed, landing his plane in Scotland. This sensational occurrence was proof positive to Ada that Hitler wished to sue for peace, and if all involved behaved sensibly the war could be over in a matter of weeks. She seemed to be trying to rope in the vicar as an ally in the face of Sudgen's continuing scepticism.

'It certainly seems that something important's afoot,' the vicar was saying.

'I shouldn't ha' thought he'd just want to be first in t'queue for t'grouse shooting,' Sudgen said, with more sarcasm than was really polite to a man of the cloth.

'What else can it mean, then?' Ada demanded.

'I don't know. But we might as well never have started if we're going to give up now.'

'Stalin's made a separate peace,' the vicar said.

'Stalin's not at war and he's got nowt to lose. Hitler's given him half o' Poland. What's he goin' to give us – that half o' France 'at he didn't occupy?'

'It's t'Russians he's really after. He wishes we'd never started.'

This from a young voice that cut through the adult babble and made them all look up. It was George Palmer. An expression of annoyance settled on Ada's face at this interjection by one of his age. She seemed to overlook that what George had just said was a view she herself had brought from her employers some time ago.

Sugden turned his head to look at his grandson. Though not as highly strung and showily clever as his younger brother Granville, George was known to be deep and thoughtful and to read a lot.

'What bothers me, George lad,' Sugden said, 'is why did we start if we're goin' to break off afore t'job's done?'

'What job's that?' Ada asked.

'Puttin' Hitler down and makin' sure he never bobs up again,' George answered her.

'I didn't ask you,' Ada said.

'He's told thee, all t'same,' Sugden said, and Ada flushed and glanced uneasily at the vicar, who had been listening and looking at everybody with a supercilious half-smile on his lips which made Ella want to ask him why, if he thought he knew better than anybody else there, he didn't put them all straight. Only, she didn't think he did know.

When she got to the ladies there was nobody in there but little Mary Butterworth's mother, a woman with fat cheeks and a feather in her hat. She looked at Ella in the glass, showing no sign of being cowed by the hard man to whom she was bound in marriage.

'What a blessing it stayed fine for it.'

'Yes, it makes a difference. There was three feet of snow on my wedding day.'

'You'd have your love to keep you warm.'

Surprised, Ella laughed. 'Aye, that an' red flannel.'

'Didn't they make a lovely couple? Didn't you think so?'

'I did.'

'Only young, Mary, but a lovely personality.'

'She obviously thinks the world of Trevor.'

'And him of her. Now, let me see, you're . . .'

'I'm Mary's auntie. Her father's youngest sister.'

'That's right. Ella.'

'Yes.'

'You work with Olive Sims.'

'I do.'

'Well, Olive's mother's my cousin, on me mother's side.'

Ella said, 'Me mother allus says 'at everybody in Daker must be related if only you could go back far enough.'

'Like t'Royal Family.'

'Aye. That's not stopped many wars, has it?'

'Brought 'em on, if you ask me.'

What with all this Ella forgot Winnie until the reception broke up on the hired premises and people began to go home or straggle up the road to Ronald and Martha's house, where they were promised more refreshment.

Sugden's leg had been troubling him and, reluctantly, he walked anywhere farther than into the garden with a stick.

'What d'you think?' Patience asked.

'Let's go,' he said. 'We can come away when we want, and we don't get together nowadays.'

Ella walked a little in front until something made her look back between her parents to where Arthur was coming along with one of Winnie's children on either hand. She retraced her steps.

'Where's Winnie?'

He shook his head and indicated the children. 'I don't know,' he said almost inaudibly.

'Where's me mam?' Linda asked. 'I want me mam.'

'I'm goin' to fetch her once I've taken you to your Auntie Martha's.'

'I can take 'em up there,' Ella said. 'But where will you go? If she'd been taken badly she'd have told somebody, wouldn't she?'

'Aye. All the same, I can only try her at home first.'

And where would he try second? That look she had seen in Winnie's eyes seemed suddenly terrifying in memory. She felt heat break through her skin from top to toe. She wanted to ask Arthur what he thought, what he knew, what he had seen and heard, but couldn't because of the children, and because she superstitiously felt that only in keeping silent was there any protection now against calamity.

162

'Arthur,' she said, 'come straight away and tell me. Don't go dashing about without me. Promise.'

He nodded. 'Promise.' He left her at a trot.

5

She was looking at the smooth flow of black water below her feet. When she stood straight she could see it between the planks of the bridge. Only just, now, though, because the light was beginning to fade. The rest of the bridge behind her was occupied by the single railway line along which coal was hauled from the pit across the canal to the hoppers, where it was shuttered into waiting lorries. She could still see the hoppers halfway between her and the bridge, and the mill where she worked; but she could no longer make out the pit in the wood, which was where Thomas had died. That was lost now in the darkness gathering in the trees surrounding it.

She was beginning to fear that complete darkness would find her here alone.

They had searched – she and Arthur – all this area of copses and riverside, all through the long dying of a glorious evening. Then they had split up, he going one way she the other, covering ground again as brightness cooled, colour withdrew with receding light and night uncoiled itself and stretched in woods, under bridges, along the walls of the few isolated builings here, and drew like a curtain along the wall of the railway cutting up whose side were the steps she must climb to reach the town.

The meandering course of the river nudged then swung away from the man-made cut of the canal. Ella had wanted to go that much farther but Arthur had said no.

'Waste of valuable time.'

'Why? We've looked everywhere else.'

'Not properly. We can't have looked properly.'

'Why couldn't she have gone across to the canal?' But she knew even as she asked, and knew him to gag on the answer.

'If she's over there she'll just be wanderin' and she's safe. It's not deep enough,' he managed then. 'Would you cross a river like this to get there, if you . . . if you . . . ?'

All the way along they had gone, downstream to the next bridge, stunned into silence by their fear as they stood in the great three-quarter circle of that loop where the pools were deepest, where the tough men-boys from the mill houses swam, where the water slid over dam-stakes and anything, anything at all of any size put into the water higher up would, except in floodtimes, eventually come to rest. And still he had returned alone, sending her upstream from the first bridge, where they knew that no one ever drowned, while he went once more along every yard of bank, in his knowledge of the places to end it all that came with the childhood lore of all brought up in the village.

But she hadn't. She wouldn't. She had no reason to.

There was nobody about now. Earlier there had been a couple, then a man on his own with a dog; and a woman alone whose saunter had made Ella run after her, only to retrace her steps when she had confirmed her mistake. Now there was no one to be seen and she was scared. She had once been foolish enough to walk home from work in the dark on her own and, ending up terrified, had vowed never to put herself into such a situation again. But the darkness closed round her and Arthur was nowhere to be seen.

She dared not move for fear they missed each other. He surely couldn't be long now. Unless, of course, he had found what he was looking for. What he – they – dreaded. She knew that they had both been swept beyond logic and probability, so that now there was only what they feared. 'She could,' the small voice said in Ella. 'Whether you think there's a reason or not, you know she could, because she's the kind who does: haunted, fated. That look, brought from a place where such as you, girl, can't follow.' Oh, Winnie, Winnie, Winnie . . .

A football on the boards startled her so violently her limbs jerked as if on strings.

'Sorry, Ella, I didn't mean to scare you.'

'I never saw you coming.' She waited. 'No . . . ?' She had nearly said 'No luck?' but checked herself in time.

'We'd better be goin'.' But he stood, his head down.

Then Ella was crying and she knew that he was too. And when she touched him he turned and came into her arms. They were near enough of an age and still only young and they clung to each other like children. His tears were salt on her cheek and hers on his.

Presently they set off towards the town. There was no light anywhere to guide them and though both of them knew the ground they trod as well as they knew any, it was uneven, full of the surprises of darkness, and Ella stumbled until Arthur drew her arm firmly through his.

They were silent as they crossed the bridge over the main railway line, the line along which she had travelled to her honeymoon, the line that brought Walter home, the line that had taken him away. Arthur stood back to let her go first up the steep, dog's-hind-leg flight of stone steps. At the top, in the ginnel leading to the first street of the village, she said on slightly laboured breath. 'What do we do now?'

'We shall have to tell the police.'

'Are you going to do that?'

'If I have to.'

'We'd best wait and see what the others have to say.'

They walked on. Near the middle of the village Arthur said, stopping, 'Look, I'm going up there again first.'

'To Winnie's?'

'Yes. I'll come to grandad's when I've been.'

'I'm coming with you.'

'If you like.'

She went dumbly along. Now he no longer held her arm and she had to take occasional trotting steps to keep up. She let him go, thinking she would meet him on his way back. There was no reason for her to rush as well. But she didn't want to go home without him. They must share the telling.

He waited for her at the end of the lane. Without

165

speaking they walked towards the dark cottage. As they drew near Arthur suddenly stopped. Ella felt his grip on her arm.

'What's up?'

'Do you notice anything?'

'No.'

'Somebody's drawn the curtains.'

'Oh!' She felt her heart flutter like a bird in a box. She went after him and was with him as he opened the door.

Gaslight greeted them. Winnie, still in her coat, turned her face to them from where, one hand resting on the mantelshelf, she had been contemplating the empty firegrate.

'Well . . .' Arthur said.

'If you knew,' Ella said, 'the places we've been lookin' for you.'

'Where've you been?' Arthur asked.

'Walkin'.'

'I should think so,' Ella said. She was on an edge of temper that relief helped to sharpen.

'I had to get away on me own,' Winnie said. The corner of her mouth lifted in a sad imitation of a smile. 'You know me and weddings.'

'We've searched high an' low.' Ella heard her own voice and hated its plaintive note. Like that of someone put out by a missed appointment. All the same, it was wicked of Winnie to frighten them like that.

'Where are me bairns?'

'Me mam'll have put 'em to bed by now.'

Winnie nodded. 'I knew they'd be looked after. They're best off where they are. It's time you were in your beds an' all.'

'I'll hang on if there's anything you want,' Arthur said.

Winnie shook her head. 'You go with Ella. I'm lockin' me door now.'

They went out. They had to. Something in Winnie herself was locked against them. It refused explanations or apologies. Relief was stirring anger in Arthur as they walked back to the road.

'I feel a fool now.'

'You're in good company.'

'I shall tell her.'

'Oh, aye. But it won't do any good. Winnie's Winnie.'
Or don't you know? she wanted to add.

What she did say after a moment was, 'Arthur, don't
you think you'd be best off breaking clear?'

'What d'you mean?'

'If you don't know I can't tell you. I've only me
thoughts to go on.'

He was silent. She felt his struggle as he trudged beside
her.

'I'd like to tell you, somebody, but it's . . .'

'It's what?'

'It's complicated.'

'What on earth's complicated about it?'

'P'raps one day I'll be able to tell you.'

'Only what you feel you can. I've only tried to advise
you for your own good.'

'Winnie's been very good to me.'

'Yes.'

'And I can't let her down.'

'No.'

'I know you're a friend as well.'

'I hope you do.'

'And you won't tell anybody else what you think you
know.'

'You can rely on that.'

He stopped in the thicker darkness at the mouth of
the lane and reached for her hands. To her surprise he
drew her to him and embraced her, putting his cheek
once more against hers. It was a boldness, she thought
later, that he could only have summoned from remem-
brance of when they had shared the tears of extreme
distress, and something pierced Ella so that she could
have wept again now.

But he stood away from her.

'You an' me,' he said, 'we know things that none of
'em know.'

Oh, I don't know, though, Ella thought. They've lived longer and seen more. But she said, 'Yes, I expect so.'

'Will you go to your own house now? I mean after you've told them?'

'No, I expect I'll get into me old bed with them bairns. They'll want their mother when they wake up.'

'I'll go back and see her first thing.'

Ella thought that she was best left to come round in her own time, but she said, 'Just as you like.'

6

So it was Arthur who found her when he went back; Arthur who broke a window to get in when he got no answer to his repeated knocks; Arthur who climbed the stairs and looked at her in her bed. She had undressed and got in under a light blanket and the bottle she had drunk from lay on the floor near her dangling hand; though after she let it fall there could have been for her no peaceful exit through the other door of sleep.

Twelve

1

'Missus . . .'

Clarice Mellor nudged her. 'It's you he wants, Ella.'

He stood to one side, out of the stream of home-going mill-girls. So far as Ella could recollect he was dressed exactly as she had seen him before.

'I'll see you later, Clarice.'

'Right. So long, then.' Clarice threw the countryman figure – 'like a poacher', he'd been described – a last curious glance and went on her way.

Ella said, 'Hullo.'

'I called to see Winnie,' Mole Templeton said. 'I couldn't find anybody at home.'

She shook her head. This was the last thing she had expected. 'You don't know, do you?'

'Know what?' But something was dawning, if not the worst.

'What's happened to her?'

Ella faced him. She felt her eyes brim.

It was enough. He said. 'Is she . . . ? She can't be . . .'

Ella nodded. 'I thought you'd know.' She meant she had hoped he would find out without coming here.

'You'd better tell me what happened, Missus.'

'She's dead.' He waited. 'She killed herself.'

She told then in a rush how Winnie had seemed down at the wedding, how she had gone missing, how she and Arthur had searched and thought her safe.

'Then what?'

'She drank some stuff in the night.'

He shook his head, as if to refuse it all a place. 'I can't believe it. I don't understand why.'

'She was a bit that way, y'know,' Ella said. 'Up an' down. She got really depressed sometimes.'

'There must have been summat else. You're not tellin' me everything.'

Ella touched his arm. 'Come on here.' There was a side path which led along the rim of the railway cutting. Thick bushes and a fence hid the drop. She and Clarice had been among the last to leave the mill, but they had passed some dawdlers who topped the steps now. She would be talked about.

'She was having a bairn.'

That silenced him. He walked a few paces then turned back. His lips moved but Ella could hear no sound.

Then, 'There was somebody else all the time.'

'Was there?'

'Did you think it was me?'

Some folk had. She had had no choice but to let them think so. Unable to give him the character she thought he deserved.

'I'd asked her to marry me. I'd a home waiting for her.'

'It's a shame,' Ella said. He had taken off his cap on first speaking to her, with that stiff country courtesy that had once amused her, and he twisted it in his hands as if he would tear it apart. 'I'm sorry,' Ella said. 'I can't tell you how sorry I am.'

'I'd've taken her husband's kids,' Mole said. 'I was ready for that.' He shook his head, looking at his boots. 'But not one she'd got while I was waiting for her.'

When Ella didn't speak he said, 'You can't blame me, can you?'

'Oh, no. Nobody can blame you.'

'I hope he burns in hell, though, when his time comes,' Mole said. 'Whoever he is, that's what he deserves.'

He raised his hand with the cap in it. Into the open cap he buried his face and she heard the muffled anguish of his voice as he said over and over again, 'Oh, dear! Oh, dear! Oh, dear!'

James saw her go into a shop and waited outside for her.

'Have you heard about our Arthur?'

It was only the smile on his face that quelled raw panic.

'What about Arthur?'

'He's joined up. The silly bugger's gone and joined the army.' He waited for her response, but she said nothing, thinking. 'T'job he wa' doin' they might never have fetched him at all,' James said.

'Is that what you're hoping for?'

His smile slipped. He couldn't read her tone.

'They need coal for t'war effort, don't they? What's point in takin' skilled colliers for t'army?'

'None. They can take anybody for that, I expect.'

James scowled. He felt got at and couldn't understand her. Nor did she feel she was being fair. What he said was true and no cause for shame. But his patronising attitude to his brother had got under her skin and in pricking his conceit she felt that she defended Arthur.

'I only hope he can stand it,' James said.

'Stand what?'

'All that square-bashin' and sergeant-majors.'

'What's he joined?'

'Koylis.'

Infantry. Foot soldiers. Up and over. Walking towards the guns. She had seen so many films.

'Is your mam upset?'

'Livid.'

'It's your dad's old regiment, isn't it?'

'Aye. He doesn't know how to take it.'

'No.' Ella sighed. 'Well, we'll just have to hope he comes home a hero. Eh?

'I think he's barmy,' James said.

Happen so, Ella thought. But you, my lad, are stupid, and that's worse.

Part Three

Thirteen

1

It had taken her a long time to confide in anyone: to
confide as distinct from confessing when challenged,
as she had to Olive and Arthur, and then as little as
necessary. Not that she was capable of telling Daisy
everything. Her feelings had gone through some changes
since it all began. But she could rely on Daisy to boil it
down. Her commonsense way of seeing through to the
essentials was what had finally decided Ella to talk to her.

Olive had brought her the letter, all of a fidget with
excitement. Some word at last, after all that time! But,
'It's not Howard's handwriting, is it?'

No. Yet it had to be about him, or why had it come
care of Olive? It hadn't come through an army post
office, either; and it had been posted in England.

'Don't say it's bad news, Ella.'

Ella tore it open. Her hands weren't steady. 'No. Not
that kind of bad news, anyway.' She was sweating, where
a minute or two ago she had been aware of a draught.

'What kind, then?'

'He's been wounded.'

'So he can't write himself?'

'No, he's all right.'

But he obviously wasn't.

She felt Olive's eyes on her most of the shift and could
not avoid her on the way home.

'Why has somebody else written?'

'Because he needs cheering up.'

'But why couldn't he write himself?'

Oh, bugger off, Olive. Why do you have to have every
last detail?

175

'Because he mustn't want to worry me.'

'Ella, he's not . . . ?'

'What?'

'He's not been blinded, has he?'

'No, he hasn't. Now shurrup, will you! Do you want everybody to know?'

But somebody else must know, she decided. She couldn't carry the burden any longer. Other people's secrets she could keep, but this one of her own she would now have to share with someone more sensible and less excitable than Olive.

Daisy called to look at the house, but flapped her hand when Ella offered to show her upstairs. 'I don't expect there's owt I haven't seen before.'

'Olive was very interested in the bed.'

Daisy laughed. 'She would be.'

'I expect you've thought we were pretty thick.' Daisy shrugged. 'You'll see why in a minute.'

Daisy lit a fag. Ella had no ashtray so she put a saucer in Daisy's lap.

'Before the war,' Ella began, 'we had a man come to stay with us twice a year. Mr Keighley. He was from Birmingham. He travelled in clocks and watches. One time he brought a young chap with him. Mr Strickland. Howard. He was showing him the ropes, so's he could take over. He was a tall, good-looking chap. We got on well together and I was looking forward to him coming again. I liked the look of him. He had lovely manners. He seemed to bring summat different with him, from somewhere else. And I thought he liked me.

'Anyway, he never did come again. Only that once. Mr Keighley told us he'd been caught stealing from the firm and he got the sack and went to jail.' Daisy pursed her lips. 'Only a short sentence, but all the same it looked as if it was over between him and me before it got started. Then the war began and Mr Keighley died.'

'But did you see him again,' Daisy said.

'Yes. It was after Dunkirk, when soldiers started coming into Daker. He spoke to me one day when I was coming out of the public library. I nearly passed out. I was with Olive. I had to tell her summat because I wanted to see him again and I couldn't do that on me own.'

'Why not?'

'I'd got married in the meantime.'

'Ah, I see. Did you still fancy him?'

'More than ever. I was nearly poorly with it.'

'So Olive covered up for you.'

'We went out in a four – me and Howard and Olive and his mate.'

'Olive 'ud like that.'

'Oh, she did. Apart from fancying Howard's mate, she could see this great romance gone wrong. Tears and broken hearts and all that.'

'Was it like that?'

'It looked like it for a while.'

'Didn't he feel the same way about you?'

'Oh, yes. Well, he reckoned he could have done, given a fair chance.' She paused. 'Nothing happened, y'know, Daisy. Nothing I couldn't tell you about.'

'But more than you'd tell your husband, eh?'

'That's different. And I ought to have said, by the way, 'at he reckoned he never did what they sent him to prison for.'

'Did you believe him?'

Ella was surprised at her hesitation, momentary though it was. 'Yes, I did.'

'What happened then?'

'They moved out and went abroad. Walter came back from Canada and I got on with married life.'

'You managed to settle to it, then?'

'I never knew how much I felt about Walter till I'd been married a while.'

'It often happens like that.'

'Y'know, Daisy, if I had my way I could wish we were all back in that last summer before the war and Walter asking me to go to the the feast with him. I thought he was a pest. I made him practically beg.'

177

'Oh, they're never any worse for that,' Daisy said airily. 'But what about this Howard?'

'Oh, I'd seen that for what it was. A young lass wantin' summat different, that looks more glamorous.'

'Well then,' Daisy said, 'it's all experience and no harm done. Where's Walter now?'

'He was in Egypt, but now Rommel's retreating again they've felt safe in shifting him to the Far East.' It was her only joke about the war. The Germans had over-run Greece and occupied Crete, a time Ella had lived through in apprehension of Walter's involvement. Hitler had invaded Russia next and savage fighting was taking place along an immense front. Walter, though farther from home, was well clear of Europe, where the Germans, with seemingly unlimited men and machines, steamrollered everything in their path.

'There's no trouble out east, is there?' Daisy asked.

'No. Thank the Lord.'

Daisy politely covered a half-yawn. 'Well, it's been nice to have a chat away from the others.'

'I haven't finished yet, though, Daisy.'

'Oh?'

'I've been getting letters from Howard, via Olive.'

'Couldn't he write to you here?'

'He doesn't know this address. Because I hadn't heard for a long time I thought he'd stopped writing. The only trouble was, I didn't know if he'd just decided to call it off or whether something was stopping him.'

'You wouldn't know, would you?' Daisy said, with sudden sympathy. 'I see it now.'

'I didn't spend all me time thinking about it. I'd enough to worry about with Walter. All the same, I did wonder.'

She came up and went to the sideboard drawer. 'Then this came.' She slid the sheet of paper out of the envelope and passed it to Daisy. 'You can read it. I'd like to know what you make of it.' She gave Daisy a moment, then said. 'He's not a doctor, is he?'

'Sounds like some sort of welfare officer. He's hoping you'll go and see Howard and get him talking again.'

'Yes.'

'What's wrong with his next of kin?'

'I don't know anything about 'em.'

'Well, they want you to go.'

'Do you get the impression it's an asylum he's in?'

'Oh, they have convalescent homes. They don't clutter their hospitals with people what have got over the worst of their injuries. What will you do?'

'I don't know. How did they find me?'

'They must have seen your letters.'

'There was nothing in 'em they couldn't read.'

'Well then.'

'Why me, though?'

'Because it seems there's nobody else. Don't you want to see him again?'

'I don't know, Daisy. That's all over.'

'Nobody's asking you to take up with him.'

'It's not what they're askin' 'at matters. They know I'm a married woman.'

Daisy thought for a minute, then shrugged. 'Happen he'll leave the army now, then he'll be all right.'

'They don't seem to think so.'

'Oh, he'll happen come round with a bit more peace and quiet.'

'I wish I thought so.'

'Well, you got over it once. Why should you risk going and stirring it all up again?'

'Why should he cheer up at the sight of me, when I can't give him anything?'

'Friendship's important.'

Ella blew air between her lips. 'Friendship! Who's going to believe that's all there is to it?'

'Is that what's really bothering you?'

'Well, you can understand it, Daisy, can't you? You live here. You know the way people think. I'd never be able to tell me mam an' dad, for a start.'

'Don't tell 'em, then,' Daisy said. 'You live on your own here now. You don't have to account for every movement.'

179

'I call in every day, though. We've still got a routine. They still know practically everywhere I go.'

'There's a war on, Ella. A lot of the old ways'll have to change. There's women working side by side with men these days. There's women going into uniform. They're not all letting men get 'em on their backs.'

'All the same, ideas'll change here at a different rate. If they change at all.'

'If you're scared of going to see this Howard because of your peace of mind, that's one thing. But I'd be buggered if I'd let tittle-tattle stop me.'

Suddenly, irresistibly, Ella was reminded of the vein of common sense she had uncovered in Winnie, which she had not known she possessed until too late. It hadn't saved her, though: Daker ways had got her in the end. She caught her breath before the tears came.

'Nay, Ella lass,' she heard Daisy say, 'it's surely not a crying matter.'

2

Autumn again. Another Christmas in sight. Twelve months since she had helped Winnie to paper her living-room, since Mole Templeton had turned up, since Arthur Palmer had jumped over a wall in the dark and scared her out of her wits.

Ella didn't expect to see Mole ever again. When she thought about him she projected him into future years, the ageing bachelor farmworker doing for himself in his tied cottage, rocking and smoking at the end of the day as he brooded about how he had so very nearly won his heart's desire.

Arthur had taken his secret with him into the army. He was in Iceland, where at certain times of the year the days never fully gave way to night, with no dark-ness to blot out shame. A country, Ella fancied, made for endless brooding. She thought now that she wouldn't be surprised whatever happened to Arthur.

It seemed to her too that she had always discerned the seeds of self-destruction in Winnie. Why then did she feel so cheated? Because there had been much more to her sister-in-law than she had realized and she was no sooner aware of it than it was snatched away? She couldn't have guessed a year ago how much she would miss her. Only her last few months had brought them close enough for Ella to know real grief for Winnie's end. She had given Winnie her friendship and guarded her secrets, but she had not been trusted with the final confidence. 'There was no need for it,' she had cried silently. Nothing in the social shame warranted that. Some of those who would have called her most harshly were contemptuous of her for not having thrown herself on their mercy. But she had not been able to. It had been too much. And Ella wondered if, without those circumstances, others would later have been drummed into serving the same purpose, so that Winnie would have killed herself one day whatever happened.

It was a bit too easy: it relieved everyone else of responsibility. Oh, Winnie! Winnie had been unlike the rest of them to the end. They weren't surprised. Shocked, perhaps, but not surprised.

Ella had been thinking a lot about the mysteries of the mind since going to see Howard Strickland.

Only Daisy Marriott knew she had been. Daisy had helped her with a story for her parents. For although Sunday was when Ella had a long lie-in, cleaned the house, occasionally went to chapel, it was still sensible to pool rations and have her dinner with Sugden and Patience. When Sugden's hens were not laying Patience still produced superb Yorkshire puddings with wartime dried egg. 'Them that eats t'most pudding get most meat,' had been the trick of pre-war poverty. For when you'd stuffed yourself with pudding your appetite was understandably less. But if poverty had been suspended for the duration, so had plenty – for the likes of them, at any rate – and a good helping of pudding kept you from dwelling too much on the present niggardly ration of meat.

181

She thought about the meat, though, and the pudding, as she opened the jam sandwiches she had brought with her in a corner of the station buffet where she waited to change trains. It was a pleasant buffet of dark polished wood, gleaming brass and copper and sparkling glass, generating nearly enough warmth to offset the frosty manner of the woman in charge. Fortunately Ella had got her cup of tea and paid for it before she took out her sandwiches. The woman's glasses flashed.

'You're not allowed to eat your own food in here.'

There was a time when Ella might have apologized and slunk away; but now she said, pointing to two or three curling pieces of bread under a glass dome, 'Is that all you've got to offer?'

'It's Sunday. We don't have fresh on a Sunday.'

'These are fresh,' Ella said. 'I thought I'd be on t'safe side.'

'All the same, we're not supposed to serve drinks with customers' own food.'

'I'll sit outside,' Ella said.

'And we don't allow cups and glasses on the platform.'

'Tell me summat you do allow,' Ella said, settling back on to the bench.

'They allow cantankerous old cows like her to make folk's lives a misery,' another voice said clearly. Ella had barely glanced at the old man with the walking-stick sitting over a gill of beer at the other end of the room, and when she turned her head now she could have thought she had only imagined that he had spoken.

'Who do you think you're talkin' to?' the woman behind the counter demanded. Ella could see that she was startled, off-balance at being attacked so directly.

'I'm talkin' about you, you cantankerous cow,' the old man said, lifting his chin slightly now.

'I'll have you put out,' the woman shrilled, but the old man cut her short with another fiercely contemptuous broadside.

'Fetch your army an' start puttin'. As if we didn't have enough to contend with, we have to listen to folk like you makin' things worse. If you're not satisfied with your husband take it out on him, don't spread it around everybody else.'

'What do you know about my husband?'

'I know nasty natures like yours usually begin at home.'

The woman's face was now one angry red flush. She lifted the counter flap. 'I don't need no army. I'll put you out meself.'

The old man lifted his stick and laid it across the table. 'Don't thee try,' he advised.

'Leave him alone,' Ella said. 'Let him finish his drink.'

'And you finish yours,' the woman said. 'Let's be rid of both of you.'

Ella could hear a train approaching. She thought it must be hers. She got up, reluctant to be seeming to obey the woman's command. The old man was rising too. He buttoned his raincoat with arthritic fingers and picked up his stick. The woman backed away as he flourished it.

'You do . . .' she began.

'Don't be such a silly cow,' the old man said. Ella held the door for him. 'Just mind you don't drown in it.'

The woman looked perplexed and couldn't resist asking. 'Drown in what?'

'The milk of human kindness,' the old man said. Ella heard him mutter it again under his breath as the door closed behind them. 'The milk of human bloody kindness.'

The train rolled in, a local stopping train, taking its time. Ella got on with the old man. They had the compartment to themselves and settled in opposite window seats.

'What an unpleasant woman,' Ella said.

The old man was selecting a handrolled fag from a number nestling in an old tobacco tin.

'I've seen her at that game before,' he said. 'Browbeating. Gerrin' away with it an' all. I bet you could eat off t'floor in her house. An' I bet her husband has to do, sometimes.'

'You seem to know a lot about her.'

'I know her sort.' The old man brooded for a moment.

183

He lit the cigarette with an ancient petrol lighter that gave out a black-tipped flame. 'I'd a daughter 'at was just such another.' He sighed, took a drag. 'I'd ha' blamed meself if I hadn't had two more 'at were as sweet as pie.'

'They can be a funny mixture, families.'

'How many is there in yours?'

'I'm t'youngest of nine. They reared six. There's five of us now. I'd a brother killed down the pit last year.'

He nodded. 'I'd just the three lasses.'

They fell silent. Ella was glad that the fine weather had held, because she was supposed to be having a day walking in the country with women from the mill. As the train stopped, then trundled on again, she said to the old man,

'I'd be glad if you'd tell me the station for Wilmington Park, if you're going that far.'

'Is it the hospital you're wanting? I'm going there meself.'

'Oh, righto.' She said after a moment. 'Is it a mental hospital?'

His glance passed across her face. 'They have a psychiatric wing, I believe.'

'I see.'

'Is it your husband?'

'Oh, no, he's abroad. No, it's a friend.'

'Mine's a grandson.'

'I hope it's nothing serious.'

'He's lost a leg.' The old man removed a dewdrop with the backs of his fingers. 'They say he'll learn to live without it.'

'You'd be too old for the last one, weren't you?' Ella said. 'Like my father.'

'Oh aye. I tried for the one before that. South Africa.'

'That was all volunteers, wasn't it?'

'Oh, yes. No conscription in them days. Rally to the flag, boys. I fancied a bit of adventure. See a Zulu or two.'

'Didn't they take you?'

'No, they said I was too old. I've been too old for every war this century.'

184

'I'd say you were lucky.'

'Aye . . . But when I look at this lad I'm goin' to see . . .' He shook his head. 'I can't describe me feelings, really.'

They got off the train and left the station together. The old man pointed with his stick. 'Twenty minutes' walk up that road there. For me, I should say. You'll do it in half the time, so get off with you and don't hang about waitin' for me.'

A few people walked ahead of her. She was sweating a little as she breasted the hill. A bus from the opposite direction dropped passengers at the park gate. Ella followed them along a winding drive through level pasture where cattle grazed and the tree trunks were protected by iron guards. As the house came into view she got her first sight also of its inmates. Their uniforms were designed to be unmistakable: patches of startling blue against the green lawns and the stained stonework of the house front. A little closer and you could make out their white shirts and the brilliant scarlet of their neckties. No mistaken white feathers for this lot when they ventured on to the streets: it was to be seen in an instant and from some way off what they were. The uniform was like a medal.

A man in a white smock over khaki sat behind a table in the big entrance hall. As visitors spoke to him he checked lists of names in front of him and gave directions. Some people, who knew where they had to go, walked straight through into other rooms and along passages. As Ella said who she had come to see a man standing to one side and behind the orderly's chair stepped forward.

'Mrs Lindley?' Ella said yes. 'I'll take care of you.' He beckoned her, smiling slightly. She walked round the table and fell in beside him. She was surprised that he was wearing the blue. 'I'm Oliver Rawlinson, by the way.'

Ella had never met anyone called Oliver. She knew of only two or three people with that name. There was Oliver Cromwell, of course, and the fat half of Laurel and Hardy. And Oliver Twist, who asked for more.

'Sergeant Rawlinson?' she asked.

'Yes. I wrote to you. Thank you for responding so promptly.'

'I didn't know you were . . . I thought you were . . .'

'You didn't know I was a patient myself, you mean? Oh, yes. I'm a friend of Howard's. We were wounded in the same action, in North Africa.' A man of middle height, in his late twenties, with slicked back dark hair and one eyelid which drooped as though drawn down by some unseeable fine though yielding thread. He spoke good English with quiet ease. Ella wondered why he wasn't an officer. 'You see,' he was saying, 'I've been a bit concerned about old Howard and when I got wind that they might be discharging me soon I thought it was time I did something about it.'

'Is he all right?' Ella asked. 'In himself, I mean.'

'That's the hardest one of all to answer,' Rawlinson said. 'If you mean is he in one piece, yes he is. He caught a nasty leg wound and there was talk apparently of taking it off. But then they pottered about remaking some bones in his thigh and restringing the muscles, as it were, and said it would be OK eventually, though he'd probably have a limp for the rest of his natural and he'd better give up any idea of being good at ball games.'

'But he's depressed, you say.'

'Yes. He's retreated right inside himself, and that's the bit that worries me.'

'Are they treating him for that as well?'

'Oh, no. They seem to think that as his physical condition improves that will clear up with it.'

'So he's not in the psychiatric wing?'

'Psychiatric wing? Who on earth told you about that?'

'I asked somebody, because I wondered.'

'No, no.'

'I just want to know what to expect.'

'Yes, of course.'

'What about his next of kin?'

'There's no one I've been able to get hold of. Howard's sister is married to a Royal Navy man. She has two small children and lives in Devon. It's hard for her to make the journey. His mother . . . she's been ill herself. I don't know anything about his father.'

They came to a halt by a heavy oak door which stood open, revealing a large recreation room full of small groupings of easy chairs, with coffee tables. Just inside the door a young woman with an anxious expression was leaning forward and grasping the hands of a man in blue.

'It's you he used to talk about,' Rawlinson said, and frowned, at a loss, when Ella said at once, 'Whatever for?'

He shook his head. 'I'm sorry . . .'

'I'm trying to imagine what he could find to say. I'm a married woman.'

'I know. I've seen your letters.'

'I can't say I like that. Even if there was nothing in them.'

'I beg your pardon, but I had to find out where to reach you.'

Ella said, 'Well . . .' into a deep sigh as she looked once more through the door at the recreation room. She couldn't see Howard among the men in there. She motioned with her hand.

'In here?'

'Across . . .'

'Why didn't he write himself?'

'He seems to have given up hope.'

'Of me? He surely did that long ago.'

'Of things in general. Of everything.' Rawlinson looked directly at her. 'It really was very important that I ask you to come.' He took her by the elbow and led her into the room. 'I think you should be able to see him before he sees you.'

There was a long glassed-in verandah attached to the back of the house, forming an extension to the recreation room. Outside was more grass and some single-storey section-built blocks which spoilt the look of the place but provided more facilities. Rawlinson guided her to a window and nodded.

'There he is.'

He sat absolutely still, his head down in his shoulders. That wonderfully luxuriant spring of wavy blond hair which had so caught her attention at first sight, and which she had felt her hand would bounce off if it touched – that was cut back to an uncombable stubble, darker, without light in it. She thought the length of his body seemed to have been arranged, folded into the wheelchair like a carpenter's jointed rule. He was skin and bone. He brought straight back to her mind her dream about the blitz and sitting next to him in the cinema while he thumped his thigh and dust rose from it in small cloud. Oh, God! but he was a long, long way from being well.

'How do you think he looks?' Rawlinson asked and she heard the escaping breath of his sigh when she said with chilling candour, 'Terrible.'

He said in a moment, 'Are you ready?'

'As I ever shall be.' As he opened the door her fingers plucked at his sleeve. 'You didn't tell him I was coming, did you?'

'No. I thought the surprise might do him good.'

She nodded. 'All right.'

He led the way now. He was big enough to shield her approach. He stood over Howard, who did not even look up as he said, 'Howard, I've brought somebody to see you.'

She stepped forward as Rawlinson moved to the far side of the chair.

'Hullo, Howard,' she said. She really made quite a good job of controlling her voice.

Fourteen

1

Get it over with, she told herself. Get it out. You're a grown woman. Married. Aye, married. None of it would matter but for that. Well, married she might be, but she didn't live in purdah. Neither had Walter locked her into a chastity belt and gone off to war with the key. She was expected to know how to behave. But, she thought, I'll make the decisions.

Her mother had just carried a shovel of fire from the living-room to the parlour. Ella followed her and watched her carefully place new coal on top of it. Ella still had her coat on. She had only just walked in.

'Are you expecting company?'

'No, but I thought it was beginning to smell a bit musty. I like to air it through now and again.'

'Is me dad lying down?'

'He said he thought he'd have a couple of hours after his dinner. He's not been too well.' Ella had thought he looked grey.

'It's bitter cold out.'

Christmas was behind them. They were on the long haul to spring.

'Where've *you* been, anyway?' Patience wanted to know. 'Where did you go dashing off to straight after your dinner?'

'I've been to Grasscommon Grange.'

'Calderford? Isn't that an army hospital now?'

'Yes.'

'Who do you know in there?'

'Howard Strickland.'

'Who?' Patience sometimes pretended to be hard of

hearing when she needed a few moments to think.

'You remember him, don't you?'

'What's he doing in there?'

'He's in the army. He was wounded in North Africa.'

'How did you know about it?'

'He wrote and told me.'

'There's been no letters here for you. How did he know where you lived?'

'Olive Sims told him.'

'How does she know him?'

'She writes to a friend of his. Another soldier.'

'Where did she meet him?'

'Here, in Daker.'

'He was stationed here?'

'Yes.'

Ella had gone much further than she had ever intended. With surprising speed her mother's questions had led to the revelation of her past deceit. After a further moment's stillness and thought the connection was made.

'Was Strickland here an' all?'

'Yes.'

'And you knew.'

'Yes. I only saw him a couple of times. I knew you'd be uneasy about him, and he wouldn't be here long, so I thought it best to say nothing.'

'It *was* him I saw that morning, then, when they were marchin' away.'

'I didn't see him then.'

'No, you were in bed with your husband, where you belonged. But you knew very well when I spoke 'at it was him.'

'Walter didn't know anything about him.'

'Does he now?'

'Not yet.'

'Are you going to tell him?'

'What is there to tell him?'

'What is there to hide?'

'Nothing.'

'Well then.'

190

'He didn't steal, you know.'

'Is that what he says?'

'Yes.'

'I'd rather believe Mr Keighley.'

'Mr Keighley only knew what he'd been told.'

'What wa' proved in a court o' law.'

'Well, I believe Howard.'

'I expect you would.'

'Mother, why do you manage in half a minute to put me in the wrong, to make me feel guilty?'

'I can't account for your conscience.'

'I've told you all there is to tell.'

'I thought you'd washed your hands of him long ago.'

'I had to go to him when I heard what had happened. He's got nobody else.'

'What about his family?'

'His sister's stuck fast down in Devon and his mother's an invalid. His father's dead. They've been very worried about him. They thought he was going to have a mental breakdown on top of everything else.'

'How long have you known about all this?'

'Three, nearly four months.'

'That's what you were so secretive about. That's where you've been sloping off to.'

'I went twice while he was in Cheshire, that's all.'

'And now he's moved on to t'doorstep.'

'Mother, it wasn't Howard himself who first wrote and told me; it was a friend who was seriously worried about him.'

A board creaked overhead. Patience said, 'That's your father gettin' up. What are you going to tell him?'

'I shall tell him nothing,' Ella said. 'You can tell him what you like. I've only told you so's you'll know if anybody else comes with it.'

The new coal was taking hold. Patience added a few more bright lumps and put the mesh guard in place. As she turned to Ella again she waved her hand from the wrist at the flicker of new flame.

'That's what you're playin' with,' she said. 'I hope

you realize. You do what you feel you have to do and don't ever let it be said I made you hard-hearted. But remember 'at you're playin' with fire.'

2

He had been outside the building this time as she walked through the gate. She couldn't be sure for a moment as she had not thought of him on his feet; but as he picked her out and began to swing towards her on his good leg, between crutches, she was taken unawares by the prick of sudden tears. For what she was seeing was more than progress towards physical recovery, he had broken the shell of that terrible imprisoning apathy.

The day was dark. There had been no sun to melt the night's frost. It lay across the grass and in castor-sugar islands on the asphalt paths. When she saw the rubber ferrule of one of Howard's crutches lose its grip she gasped and quickened her step, still hurrying as he recovered his balance and stood waiting for her. He smiled then and she remembered with a small but distinct tremor of the heart that she had not seen him smile so openly, with the whole face, since the first time he came to Daker. They had been to see Robert Donat and Marlene Dietrich at the local pictures and he had taken fish and chips and bottled beer back to the house as a last-night treat. He was the most romantic man she had ever laid eyes on in the flesh, and she was going to be very patient until he came again . . .

Leaning forward on his crutches he took both her hands in his. 'Where's your gloves?' she cried. 'Your hands are frozen.'

He was smiling quietly now, his eyes on her face. 'Oh, in my pocket, I expect.' As she made to get them he said, 'Don't bother, we'll be going inside,' and Ella drew back, aware that in her impulsive reach for his pockets she had taken familiarity a small step further.

She walked behind him when he swung round and made for the redbrick building.

'How do you think I look?' he asked.

'Wonderful!' Ella said, and added, 'Compared.'

'Yes, compared. Compared with the wreck I was when you first visited me.' It was seeing him in that state which had cured her of her shyness towards him. She knew now without a doubt that she was the stronger of the two of them and that everything must be weighed and decided in that knowledge. 'I've come a long way since then, Ella, and you've been the most important thing in that. Oh, yes, you have,' he insisted when she made a dismissive gesture. 'And it gets better all the time.'

They were at the foot of the wide stone steps leading to the front door. A board had been secured across a part of their width to make a ramp for wheelchairs. Howard stopped and faced her, taking her hand again.

'I'll bet you were quite surprised when you knew I was here,' he said.

'Flabbergasted.'

'Were you pleased, though?'

'If I'm part of your cure I suppose I must be.' She nodded towards the open door of the house. Through glass inner doors she could see lights already burning. 'Is it any warmer inside?'

'Sorry! Yes.'

'Can you manage the steps?'

'Oh, yes. Just stand clear so's I don't accidentally clout you with a crutch.'

She watched him as he swung himself up the steps in front of her. According to Rawlinson the doctors had said he would end up with no more than a limp, and she wondered how much fobbing off there had been in that prediction. Howard had brushed her question aside the last time she had seen him, referring airily to a 'bit of foreign matter' they had had to get out. She didn't tell him how vividly Rawlinson had described it.

A nurse whose face Ella vaguely recognized was coming through the door, wearing a cape over her uniform. She held the door for them and smiled in acknowledgement of Ella's thank you.

This house had a large entrance hall too, though it was of a different architectural style and period from Wilmington Park. Ella thought it was shabbier as well, a bit more scuffed at the edges, and the heating system smelled of gas that was not being fully burnt. It was warm enough, though, where Howard led her, an open area at the end of a corridor, with chairs placed so that he could sit facing her, and no one nearer than fifteen or twenty feet to hear what they said. She helped him off with his khaki greatcoat. There was one chair more upright, with a higher, firmer seat, than the others and Howard took this so that his bad leg could stick straight out before him.

'Is it in plaster again?' Ella asked.

'For a little while.'

'How long do they reckon they'll have to keep you?'

'As soon as I can become an out-patient they'll discharge me.'

'From the army?'

'Yes.'

'Will you be sorry?'

'Desperately,' he said. 'I was just longing to get back into the fighting.' Her quick look caught the little smile.

'You're telling fibs.'

'Yes. All that's over for me. I'm just thankful I've come through it no worse than this.'

'I hope a lot more can live to say the same.'

'Yes. You must be constantly worried about your husband.'

'There was no fighting when he went out to the Far East.'

'We're talking about vast sub-continents, though, you know. Millions of square miles. There's no reason to suppose he'll ever get near any actual fighting.'

'It's what I keep tellin' meself.'

'Apart from that, the Japs coming into the war has changed everything.'

'It's spread it farther, anyway.'

'No, but they've brought the Americans in and that

194

means we can be pretty sure for the first time that we shan't lose. Not in the end, we shan't.'

'That's what my landlord says. Loopy Lockwood.'

Howard laughed. 'Loopy? Is he loopy?'

'No, he's just a bit – what d'you call it? – eccentric. Is that right?'

'I expect so. Does he do anthing besides being a landlord?'

'He sells secondhand furniture.'

'Well, if he'd lived in a house as big as this I suppose he would have been called eccentric. Eccentric Lockwood.'

Ella laughed. 'He's not daft, though.'

'He doesn't sound it. Does he own the house you live in now?'

'Yes.'

'Do you think he might have something suitable for me?'

'You can't come and live in Daker,' Ella said at once.

'Why not?'

'You know why not.'

'No . . . I expect that would be . . . I could live here, though, in Calderford. It's a pleasant enough town, with a good range of trades and industry.'

'Aren't you going back to Birmingham?'

'There's nothing in Birmingham for me.'

'What is there here?'

He said, 'Did you make your hat yourself?'

'I knitted it, yes.' It was of heather-mixture wool, close-fitting, and cosy on a day like this.

'It suits you.'

'Thank you.'

'You've had your hair cut as well.'

'It's been like this for months.'

'It's shorter than when I knew you before, though.'

'Oh, yes.'

'It shows up the shape of your face.'

'Oh.'

'Some faces couldn't stand that. Some faces would look too hard.'

She couldn't help it; she felt the colour rising under

195

the intensity of his gaze. Nor, for the moment, could she think of a single sensible thing to say.

'I'd made up my mind never to write to you again,' Howard said.

'Had you?'

'You hadn't had a letter for a long time. You must have wondered.'

'You'd better blame your friend, then.'

'For interfering?'

'If you want to call it that.'

'It did the trick, though.'

'I hope you're not blaming me for the state of mind I found you in.'

'I'm not blaming you for anything.'

'There was more to it than just moping over me, wasn't there?'

'Perhaps there was. But it was you who brought me round.'

'You'll have to face it on your own, sooner or later.'

'If I found a place to live here, and a job, I could perhaps put that off.'

Now, determinedly, Ella returned his gaze.

'Nothing's changed, y'know, Howard. You'd better not start expecting anything, because I've no more to give you than I had before.'

'Oh, but you have, Ella. You've shown you have.'

3

The Japanese air force had sunk the American fleet at Pearl Harbor. We had lost two of our best battleships, the Prince of Wales and the Repulse. Japanese armies were swarming all over the Far East. They had captured Singapore and were driving through Burma and Malaya with the same unstoppable momentum the Germans had shown in Europe. Those who remembered Japanese atrocities in China trembled now to think how eighty thousand Commonwealth servicemen taken prisoner might be treated. British forces were once again in retreat in North Africa. The Germans were still gaining ground on the Russian front.

A fine time, Ella thought, for optimism.

She knew and coped with the understandable fears of the day; but the lonely terrors of the night were what she had come to dread, when she would start out of sleep in a sweating panic, at the mercy of a totally malignant universe in which all human happiness was doomed and every loved one a hostage. A monstrous game was afoot and no person of good will could possibly grasp its rules. You could contemplate awe-struck the senseless slaughter of the First World War; but in this one evil itself had been unleashed to roam the planet.

Admitting to herself, though to no one else, that she did not like living alone, she kept as busy as possible so that she would have less time to dwell on it. She liked to take Linda and Brian out, to give them a treat and relieve Martha for a while. The children were living with Ronald and Martha, who had been granted custody by the court. Martha had surprised everybody, including her husband, when she announced that she would take them in. With Mary married and Arthur gone into the army she had the room and her hands weren't so full. Ronald asked if he was never going to be allowed a bit of peace and quiet while he was young enough to enjoy it. They had all held their breath then, waiting for him to dig in his heels, and were relieved when, having grumbled, he capitulated with no more struggle. The rest of them were either unable or unwilling, which would not have helped bad conscience had they let their brother's children go into care and be separated. None of them referred to them as Winnie's: they were always Thomas's bairns.

If Brian got upset he was apt to cry for his mother, when Linda would tell him straight out that she was never coming back and Auntie Martha was his mother now. Linda was turned five and had been going to school for six months. Their special liking was for tea at their grandmother's after a Saturday matinée at the pictures – the tuppenny rush – with dolly mixtures and jelly babies, and Ella found sitting and watching Flash Gordon, Buck Rogers and Hopalong Cassidy among the near-pandemonium of three hundred children a change from her own four silent walls.

Sugden and Patience were at their best with their two youngest grandchildren: tolerant, loving, sometimes indulgent. They brought into the house an energy, an edge of tension which, for a time at any rate, rejuvenated the old couple. Linda's especial pleasure was to read to her grandma from her picture book, Brian's to be taken in the last of the daylight to visit his grandad's hens. If they were laying and he could put in his hand for the first touch of the warm eggs he bubbled with delight. Soft-boiled eggs would likely as not be a part of their tea, with strips of buttered toast to dip in, cut from the slices Brian held to the fire on the end of the long fork.

Watching them – the absorbed pleasure of the little ones, the flush in Patience's cheeks, the rare crack of Sugden's face into an open smile – Ella felt drawn back into the secure heart of her own childhood, safe in the haven of the family, remembering feasts and parties and sharing beds with other children, warm all over in those giggling caves under blankets and quilt, not just on one side at a time. Adam, Doris, Thomas were still at home. Pantomimes, Christmas mornings. The world still with snow. Summer outings. Day trips to the seaside. New clothes at Whitsun, walking with the Whitsuntide procession, all the chapels in the district, the banners, the bands, the games in the field, mugs of tea and bottles of pop, potted-meat sandwiches, iced buns. Thomas outnumbered by his three sisters, but waited on like a lord, with two women besides his mother to cook, clean, polish and mend, and a younger one to fetch and carry. 'Where are me boots, Ella? Fetch us me collar stud. Nip to t'shop an' get us five Woodbines. Tell 'em they're for me.' Later, for a while, it was 'Can you lend us a bob, Ella? I'm skint till pay-day.'

And here now were his parentless children.

It was in Linda's face that Ella saw at certain moments the most arresting resemblance to her dead brother; and since Thomas had been closest in looks to Ronald, Linda had been taken in the street, by someone who didn't know them, for his own late child.

'You should have seen him preening himself,' Martha said. 'It put a right twinkle in his eye.'

'Oh,' Ronald said, 'there's many a chap my age . . .'

'Oh, is there?' Martha said.

'I'm no older than me father when our Ella were born.'

'Aye, but I'm not your mother. I've finished with all that.'

'Nay, not all of it, lass.'

Ella thought her sister-in-law looked suddenly bashful then, as she said, 'You know what I'm talking about.'

'We all know what tha're talkin' about,' Ronald said with deliberate mischief. 'Are tha plannin' on puttin' me out to grass?'

'Except for birthdays, anniversaries and public holidays,' Martha said, with such quick and unexpected wit that Ella burst out laughing and Ronald's face slipped into a sheepish grin.

What humour Ronald possessed Ella always recalled as rough and wounding. James had inherited this way. With the children he was good-natured but heavy handed and loud. But the little ones had softened Ronald, Linda in particular. 'She can wind him round her little finger,' Martha said. For while Linda would eye James warily; she had no fear of Ronald at all. When she climbed up to stand on his thighs, as he sat, holding an ear in each hand while she leaned in close to whisper, she was in complete command. 'How do you think they look?' Martha would ask, and Ella would always reply:

'Grand. They've landed on their feet, them two.'

Martha was on her own when Ella took them back this Saturday. She sat by the fire, reading the local paper. The table was laid. Ronald and James had gone to a Rugby League match in Calderford, and should have been back some time ago.

'They've found a pub open,' Martha said. 'That'll be

where they are. Anyway, I've had mine and they can get their own when they come.' She looked at Brian, whose jaws were working. 'Are you still eating, young man?'

'It's his grandad's chewing gum,' Ella said. 'He knows where to find it now.'

Sugden had found that the twist he smoked was upsetting his stomach. Since he didn't like ordinary pipe tobacco he had cut down and taken to chewing gum. When he tired of that he would park it under a projection of the fireplace. There, one day, Brian had found the hardened lump and popped it into his own mouth.

'It's good of you to take 'em off me hands for a while,' Martha said.

'Not as good as you takin' 'em in in the first place.'

'Oh, I get me reward a dozen times a day. And you've seen how Ronald thrives on it.' She glanced round at Brian, who had climbed on to a chair and was reaching for the cakestand. 'Here, young man, if you want a bun, ask for it. Didn't your grandma give you enough to eat? Well, there's one for you and one for Linda. And eat 'em here where I can see the crumbs before you go up for your night-clothes.' In a minute or two she sent them upstairs. 'Go and get your things and when you're undressed you can play down here while I put a hot-water bottle in your bed.'

She said to Ella when they had left the room, 'You'd got very fond of Winnie towards the end, hadn't you?'

'H'mm. I thought she improved for knowing.'

'Happen so.' She looked at Ella. 'Did you ever get to know who the chap was?'

She had never brought this up before. Ella said, 'I thought everybody had pinned it on Templeton, what come visiting from where she'd worked.'

'Oh, I never entertained that for more than two minutes,' Martha said.

'Didn't you?'

'No, I could see no sense in that at all.'

'Sense was the last thing in any of it,' Ella could not resist saying.

They were quiet. The children squealed on the landing. Ella, looking into the glowing heart of the fire, felt Martha's gaze drawn back to her.

'Kids come out with some odd things at times, don't they?'

'Like what?' Ella said.

'Oh . . . I always thought you knew more than you were letting on.'

'Nay, Martha,' Ella said. 'Winnie an' me were friendly, but she only ever told me what she wanted me to know.'

'And you wouldn't tell if you did know, would you?'

'If I thought it might do somebody some good, I might.'

Their eyes met again and parted. The children ran in.

4

She knows, Ella thought. Or she's started wondering. Something one of the kids had let drop had set her off. All she's got to do is wait, then; they'll say something else. Or perhaps she suspected before, which could be one reason for her taking in Winnie's kids.

There was a moon. She could see to walk home at a brisk pace. A figure rounded the corner of the Temperance Hall; a woman who came to meet her as she approached. 'Ella.' It was Olive Sims.

'I've just been to your house.'

'Oh?'

'I wanted to see you.'

'What about?'

'Are you going on home now?'

'Yes.'

'I'd prefer to talk inside.'

Ella would rather have got rid of her on the street. Once indoors she was capable of sitting down and gossiping for hours.

'Is it that important?'

'It's personal.'

'Oh, well then.'

They went into the house. Ella carefully closed the curtains before switching on the light. She had a coal fire today. She had damped it with slack before going out. Now she put a poker under the partly welded mass and lifted, seeing the smoke thicken as the draught got in. There would be flames in a minute or two. Olive stood holding her hands together just inside the in-door. Ella waved her to a chair hoping she wouldn't take her coat off. She kept her own on to discourage her.

'Well, it must be important if it can't keep till Monday. But why didn't you tell me this morning?'

'I didn't know this morning. And it's Sunday tomorrow.'

'All day.'

'Sunday afternoon's hospital visiting time.'

'Oh, I see.' Olive's expression was reproachful.

'Howard Strickland's in Grasscommon Grange, isn't he?'

'Yes.'

'A girl I know, a nurse there, told me she'd seen you visiting.'

'So . . . ?'

'I do think you've got an underhand way with you, Ella.'

'Underhand? Isn't that when you're trying to deceive people?'

'Well, secretive.'

'You knew I'd been to see Howard at Wilmington Park.'

'But not that he'd moved here.'

'I only found out meself a fortnight ago.'

'And you just never thought to mention it.'

'Well, to tell you the truth, I thought I'd better tell my parents first, in case anybody else did.'

'They know now, then?'

'Only just.'

'I expect they'd wonder why he'd turned up only a thre'penny bus-ride away.'

'Oh, we skated round that one.'

'Did he wangle it himself?'

'Yes. He asked for a move. He said he wanted to settle in this area when they discharged him.'

'He still fancies his chances, doesn't he?'

'You'd better ask him that. I've got a husband.'

'He does, though,' Olive said.

'Well, suppose he does? What reason is that for you to get upset?' She didn't know why, but she was uneasy, on edge. She wanted rid of Olive.

'After all I've done for you.'

Ella sighed. 'Yes, you've been a good friend, Olive. But I wish you'd tell me what's troubling you.'

'I came to ask you if you'd take me with you, to see him.'

'Howard?'

'Yes. Are you going tomorrow?'

'I thought I might.'

'Don't you go every week?'

'I didn't go last week.'

'Why do you keep him danglin'?'

'Why don't you mind you own business?'

'Will you take me with you? I won't stop all the time.'

'What do you want to see him for?'

'I want to talk to him about Tony.'

'Is there something wrong with him?'

'He's stopped writin'.'

'Do you think Howard hears from him?'

'I don't know. Do you?'

'No. He's never said.'

'But he could talk to me about him, tell me how he seemed when they were together. P'raps he'd agree to write and tell Tony 'at I'm worried.'

'All right.'

'Will you take me?'

'Yes. Meet me at the bus-stop by the Primitive Methodist Chapel at half-past one.'

'Right. Thanks, Ella. I knew you'd help me when you knew. I mean, we're all in this lot together, aren't we? Except that if anything did happen to Tony I'd have no way of knowing, would I? They'd notify his next of kin and as far as I was concerned he'd just have disappeared.'

Ella just wished that Olive would stop talking in this vein. She couldn't tell why her nerves were so on edge, but she felt worse every minute that Olive lingered.

'Well, let's hope it never comes to that,' Ella said. 'But if they found your letters among his things surely somebody would get in touch. So,' she said heartily, standing as she thought that Olive's eyes were about to fill with tears, 'I'd say that no news is good news. Well at least, it's not that kind of bad news.'

She saw her into the lobby, switched on the bottom light so that Olive could find the door handle and said, 'I shall have to switch it off again before you open the door.'

But in that few seconds of illumination, as Olive's foot caught the mat, she it was who stooped and drew out the envelope which had been concealed there.

'Post.'

'When did that come, I wonder?'

'Forces mail. News from Walter. Probably came second delivery while you were at work. You walked in, kicked the mat and covered it up.'

Yes. Ella had turned into the room again. Olive followed her with her insatiable curiosity as she said, 'It's not from Walter.' She was opening it. The important bits were quickly taken in. She sat down. If she had not done so she would have fallen. 'It's his . . . his CO.' She gasped and choked.

Olive took the paper from her fingers. The key words danced in Ella's mind: '. . . missing while on duty . . . not an operational flight . . . experienced pilot . . . no trace . . . difficult jungle terrain . . . write again as soon as I have more news . . .'

'Oh, Ella,' Olive said. Ella made no more sound. She felt as if her chest were in an enormous clasp that tightened until she could do no more than fight for each small breath. Olive it was then whose keening cry broke free, an anguished wail that chilled Ella with its horror, breaking out and rising to a pitch that it seemed would never subside. Until it finally did fall into a chant of sympathetic woe – 'Oh, Ella, Ella, Ella, Ella' – only a part of which Ella heard as her brain seemed to empty in a rushing loss of sustaining blood and for some minutes she mercifully knew nothing.

Fifteen

Dear Howard,

Thank you for your letter. I brought it here with me so that I could reply in peace. I am having a few days by the sea with Linda and Brian, my youngest brother's children. It is the school holidays. Linda has been going to school for a year now and Brian starts in two weeks.

I am glad to hear that your leg seems to be properly better at last. You have had a terrible time with it. You must have thought the pain and worry would never end.

Yes, my mother told me you had been to try to see me before they moved you down south. I was away. My sister-in-law has some relations with a farm in the Lake District and everybody thought it would be a good idea if I went away for a change. At such times you do not know whether you want people you know around you or if you are better off alone with your thoughts and memories. I had never been in the Lake District. It is a beautiful place. Not only the lakes and mountains but all the different shades of green in the trees. More than I ever imagined.

I guess from the way she talked that my mother was a bit short with you. She belongs to a different generation and upbringing. She still remembers what Mr Keighley told us, although I have told her it was all a dreadful mistake, and she did not like me visiting you in hospital while Walter was away. There is also a fitting and decent way for a widow to behave and it does not involve mixing with single men so soon after a husband's death. She remembers all the women who remained spinsters after the last war when their men were killed and there were not enough left to go round afterwards. Thank the Lord that does not look like happening this time, I mean the immense slaughter, which is one mercy in a time when there is no daylight, and it does not seem to apply to the Russians, from what we can gather they are being killed in their millions and Germans with them. How they can hope to win with so many losses, though there is as yet no end anywhere in sight.

They began to pay me a pension for Walter which proves to me that they have no hope. They would not be paying money over if they were not certain.

It is hard to describe how these last few months have passed. I have lived from day to day. People try not to mention the name of somebody who has gone, but I have tried to speak his name out loud whenever a thought of him came into my mind and it was the kind of thing I could share, without being an intimate memory of something private. To lock him up in our separate thoughts is the worst thing we could do, as if we were all pretending he never existed.

I would not have believed even three years ago what a hole he could leave in my life and an emptiness inside me. There are some things I discovered with him that I do not feel now I could ever find again with another man, or wish to know about.

I sat down the other day and thought out how many times you and I have met. Only nine times in all – if the five days you spent on your first visit with Mr Keighley are counted as one. It is very little for learning to know somebody although I have to confess that I knew Walter for years by sight and to speak to and I never knew him at all until we were married. And of course most of our married life was spent apart.

Sometimes I feel as if there is nothing but pain and sadness in this world, hopes that are dashed, treasures you find only to have them snatched away. Don't build up on anything because it is bound to go wrong.

It is good for me to be with the children. They have lost both father and mother but they are young enough to forget and be happy. Their father died in the pit, their mother killed herself in despair. It is useless to say that she should not have done it because we all loved her, because we didn't, or not enough, and she didn't know it or believe it in any case which amounts to the same thing. So it is our duty to try and make her children happy even if we cannot protect them from what life might have in store for them later.

Have you ever been to Southport? I think you would like it. It is your sort of place. When I said I would take the children to the seaside they said why didn't I go to Blackpool? But Walter and I spent our honeymoon there and apart from that Blackpool is what I think of as Walter's place, while this is more yours.

There are lovely gardens all along Lord Street and shops you can walk end to end under shelter. They had a military band in the gardens yesterday though they have no lights in the trees or in the shop windows after dark. Some people don't care for it because the sea stays so far out, but there are lakes and ponds along the front where the children can paddle and sail their boats while grownups sit in peace in the sunshine. There is even a front garden with a lawn to the boarding house where we are staying which is something you don't find in Blackpool which is street after street of lodgings with no more than steps to the pavement. Yesterday I saw my first American soldier, a tubby little chap with a fat bottom in tight trousers. His uniform was made of much better material than our boys, but I think they should have sent Gary Cooper if they intend to win the war for us.

You feel that we need something wonderful to happen to make everybody feel better, something like the Battle of Britain. They even tried a vote of no confidence in Mr Churchill though it didn't come off. He is not the kind of man colliers think much to in peacetime, but who else is there to lead us now?

The children are laughing in the garden. Brian sometimes laughs so much I think he will be sick. Linda can sometimes be a bit sly with him and I have to watch her. She is older and knows more and she has this little streak in her that needs to be looked out for.

I can hear them (I can see them if I get up) from the front room where I am writing this. Mrs Stapleton has just brought me a cup of tea from her own pot. She is a very pleasant woman with a lovely Lancashire accent that reminds me of Gracie Fields though her voice is softer and rounder. There are not many boarding houses where you are allowed to hang about inside between meals. Mostly they turn you out into the street whatever the weather. I expect you don't know all that.

I have just read over what I have written. I did not set out to write so much and I am tempted to cross some of it out and make another copy, not because it is too long but because of some of the things I have said and perhaps should have left out. But it has done me good to write so much and my thoughts are clearer for it. I hope my chatting on will not bore you.

I am going to sign off now and take the children to the sea. If and when you can get up north again please let me know. It is no use pretending Howard that I am still the girl you first met, I have lived too much for that. But I should like to see you. Not just now, but I shall want to as time goes by. We must all give each other what we can in this time of trial. It is the only way we shall ever get through.

With every good wish for your future health and happiness.

Yours sincerely
Ella (Lindley)

THE END